Bret Harte

A Protégée of Jack Hamlin's

And other stories

Bret Harte

A Protégée of Jack Hamlin's
And other stories

ISBN/EAN: 9783744747806

Printed in Europe, USA, Canada, Australia, Japan

Cover: Foto ©Andreas Hilbeck / pixelio.de

More available books at **www.hansebooks.com**

A PROTÉGÉE OF JACK HAMLIN'S

AND OTHER STORIES

BY

BRET HARTE

BOSTON AND NEW YORK
HOUGHTON, MIFFLIN AND COMPANY
The Riverside Press, Cambridge
1894

Copyright, 1894,
By BRET HARTE.

All rights reserved.

The Riverside Press, Cambridge, Mass., U.S.A.
Electrotyped and Printed by H. O. Houghton and Company.

CONTENTS.

	PAGE
A Protégée of Jack Hamlin's	1
An Ingénue of the Sierras	58
The Reformation of James Reddy	93
The Heir of the McHulishes	154
An Episode of West Woodlands	221
The Home-Coming of Jim Wilkes	272

A PROTÉGÉE OF JACK HAMLIN'S.

I.

THE steamer Silveropolis was sharply and steadily cleaving the broad, placid shallows of the Sacramento River. A large wave like an eagre, diverging from its bow, was extending to either bank, swamping the tules and threatening to submerge the lower levees. The great boat itself — a vast but delicate structure of airy stories, hanging galleries, fragile colonnades, gilded cornices, and resplendent frescoes — was throbbing throughout its whole perilous length with the pulse of high pressure and the strong monotonous beat of a powerful piston. Floods of foam pouring from the high paddle - boxes on either side and re-uniting in the wake of the boat left behind a track of dazzling whiteness, over which trailed two dense black banners flung from its lofty smokestacks.

Mr. Jack Hamlin had quietly emerged from his stateroom on deck and was looking over the guards. His hands were resting lightly on his hips over the delicate curves of his white waistcoat, and he was whistling softly, possibly some air to which he had made certain card-playing passengers dance the night before. He was in comfortable case, and his soft brown eyes under their long lashes were veiled with gentle tolerance of all things. He glanced lazily along the empty hurricane deck forward; he glanced lazily down to the saloon deck below him. Far out against the guards below him leaned a young girl. Mr. Hamlin knitted his brows slightly.

He remembered her at once. She had come on board that morning with one Ned Stratton, a brother gambler, but neither a favorite nor intimate of Jack's. From certain indications in the pair, Jack had inferred that she was some foolish or reckless creature whom "Ed" had "got on a string," and was spiriting away from her friends and family. With the abstract morality of this situation Jack was not in the least concerned. For himself he did not indulge in that sort of game; the inexperience and vacillations of innocence were apt to be bothersome, and besides, a certain modest doubt of his own competency to make an original selection had always made him prefer to confine his gallantries to the wives of men of greater judgment than himself who had.   But it suddenly occurred to him that he had seen Stratton quickly slip off the boat at the last landing stage.   Ah! that was it; he had cast away and deserted her. It was an old story.   Jack smiled.   But he was not greatly amused with Stratton.

She was very pale, and seemed to be clinging to the network railing, as if to support herself, although she was gazing fixedly at the yellow glancing current below, which seemed to be sucked down and swallowed in the paddle-box as the boat swept on.   It certainly was a fascinating sight — this sloping rapid, hurrying on to bury itself under the crushing wheels.   For a brief moment Jack saw how they would seize anything floating on that ghastly incline, whirl it round in one awful revolution of the beating paddles, and then bury it, broken and shattered out of all recognition, deep in the muddy undercurrent of the stream behind them.

She moved away presently with an odd, stiff step, chafing her gloved hands together as if they had become stiffened too in her rigid grasp of the railing. Jack leisurely watched her as she moved along the narrow strip of deck. She was not at all to his taste, — a rather plump girl with a rustic manner and a great deal of brown hair under her straw hat. She might have looked better had she not been so haggard. When she reached the door of the saloon she paused, and then, turning suddenly, began to walk quickly back again. As she neared the spot where she had been standing her pace slackened, and when she reached the railing she seemed to relapse against it in her former helpless fashion. Jack became lazily interested. Suddenly she lifted her head and cast a quick glance around and above her. In that momentary lifting of her face Jack saw her expression. Whatever it was, his own changed instantly; the next moment there was a crash on the lower deck. It was Jack who had swung himself over the rail and dropped ten feet, to her side. But not before she had placed one foot in the meshes of the netting and had gripped the railing for a spring.

The noise of Jack's fall might have seemed to her bewildered fancy as a part of her frantic act, for she fell forward vacantly on the railing. But by this time Jack had grasped her arm as if to help himself to his feet.

"I might have killed myself by that foolin', might n't I?" he said cheerfully.

The sound of a voice so near her seemed to recall to her dazed sense the uncompleted action his fall had arrested. She made a convulsive bound towards the railing, but Jack held her fast.

"Don't," he said in a low voice, "don't, it won't pay. It's the sickest game that ever was played by man or woman. Come here!"

He drew her towards an empty state-room whose door was swinging on its hinges a few feet from them. She was trembling violently; he half led, half pushed her into the room, closed the door and stood with his back against it as she dropped into a chair. She looked at him vacantly; the agitation she was undergoing inwardly had left her no sense of outward perception.

"You know Stratton would be awfully riled," continued Jack easily. "He's just stepped out to see a friend and got left by the fool boat. He 'll be along by the next steamer, and you 're bound to meet him in Sacramento."

Her staring eyes seemed suddenly to grasp his meaning. But to his surprise she burst out with a certain hysterical desperation, "No! no! Never! *never* again! Let me pass! I must go," and struggled to regain the door. Jack, albeit singularly relieved to know that she shared his private sentiments regarding Stratton, nevertheless resisted her. Whereat she suddenly turned white, reeled back, and sank in a dead faint in the chair.

The gambler turned, drew the key from the inside of the door, passed out, locking it behind him, and walked leisurely into the main saloon. "Mrs. Johnson," he said gravely, addressing the stewardess, a tall mulatto, with his usual winsome supremacy over dependents and children, "you 'll oblige me if you 'll corral a few smelling salts, vinaigrettes, hairpins, and violet powder, and unload them in deck stateroom No. 257. There 's a lady" —

"A lady, Marse Hamlin?" interrupted the mulatto, with an archly significant flash of her white teeth.

"A lady," continued Jack with unabashed gravity, "in a sort of conniption fit. A relative of mine; in fact a niece, my only sister's child. Had n't seen each other for ten years, and it was too much for her."

The woman glanced at him with a mingling of incredulous belief, but delighted obedience, hurriedly gathered a few articles from her cabin, and followed him to No. 257. The young girl was still unconscious. The stewardess applied a few restoratives with the skill of long experience, and the young girl opened her eyes. They turned vacantly from the stewardess to Jack with a look of half recognition and half frightened inquiry. "Yes," said Jack, addressing the eyes, although ostentatiously speaking to Mrs. Johnson, "she 'd only just come by steamer to 'Frisco and was n't expecting to see me, and we dropped right into each other here on the boat. And I have n't seen her since she was so high. Sister Mary ought to have warned me by letter; but she was always a slouch at letter writing. There, that 'll do, Mrs. Johnson. She 's coming round; I reckon I can manage the rest. But you go now and tell the purser I want one of those inside staterooms for my niece, — *my niece*, you hear, — so that you can be near her and look after her."

As the stewardess turned obediently away the young girl attempted to rise, but Jack checked her. "No," he said, almost brusquely; "you and I have some talking to do before she gets back, and we 've no time for foolin'. You heard what I told her just now! Well, it 's got to be as I said, you *sabe*. As long as you 're on this boat you 're my niece, and my sister Mary's child. As I have n't got any sister Mary, you don't run any risk of falling foul of her, and you ain't taking any one's place. That settles that. Now, do you or do you not want to see that man again? Say yes, and if he 's anywhere above ground I 'll yank him over to you as soon as we touch shore." He had no idea of interfering with his colleague's amours, but he had determined to make Stratton pay for the bother their slovenly sequence had caused him. Yet he was relieved and astonished by her frantic gesture of indignation and abhorrence. " No ? " he repeated grimly. "Well, that settles that. Now, look here;

quick, before she comes — do you want to go back home to your friends?"

But here occurred what he had dreaded most and probably thought he had escaped. She had stared at him, at the stewardess, at the walls, with abstracted, vacant, and bewildered, but always undimmed and unmoistened eyes. A sudden convulsion shook her whole frame, her blank expression broke like a shattered mirror, she threw her hands over her eyes and fell forward with her face to the back of her chair in an outburst of tears.

Alas for Jack! with the breaking up of those sealed fountains came her speech also, at first disconnected and incoherent, and then despairing and passionate. No! she had no longer friends or home! She had lost and disgraced them! She had disgraced *herself!* There was no home for her but the grave. Why had Jack snatched her from it? Then, bit by bit, she yielded up her story, — a story decidedly commonplace to Jack, uninteresting, and even irritating to his fastidiousness. She was a schoolgirl (not even a convent girl, but the inmate of a Presbyterian female academy at Napa. Jack shuddered as he remembered to have once seen certain of the pupils walking with a teacher), and she lived with her married sister. She had seen Stratton while going to and fro on the San Francisco boat; she had exchanged notes with him, had met him secretly, and finally consented to elope with him to Sacramento, only to discover when the boat had left the wharf the real nature of his intentions. Jack listened with infinite weariness and inward chafing. He had read all this before in cheap novelettes, in the police reports, in the Sunday papers; he had heard a street preacher declaim against it, and warn young women of the serpent-like wiles of tempters of the Stratton variety. But even now Jack failed to recognize Stratton as a serpent, or indeed anything but a blundering cheat and clown, who had left his dirty 'prentice work on his (Jack's) hands. But the girl was helpless and, it seemed, homeless, all through a certain desperation of feeling which, in spite of her tears, he could not but respect. That momentary shadow of death had exalted her. He stroked his mustache, pulled down his white waistcoat and her cry, without saying anything. He did not know that this most objectionable phase of her misery was her salvation and his own.

But the stewardess would return in a moment. "You 'd better tell me what to call you," he said quietly. "I ought to know my niece's first name."

The girl caught her breath, and, between two sobs, said, "Sophonisba."

Jack winced. It seemed only to need this last sentimental touch to complete the idiotic situation. "I 'll call you Sophy," he said hurriedly and with an effort. "And now look here! You are going in that cabin with Mrs. Johnson where she can look after you, but I can't. So I 'll have to take your word, for I 'm not going to give you away before Mrs. Johnson, that you won't try that foolishness — you know what I mean — before I see you again. Can I trust you?"

With her head still bowed over the chair back, she murmured slowly somewhere from under her disheveled hair: —

"Yes."

"Honest Injin?" adjured Jack gravely.

"Yes."

The shuffling step of the stewardess was heard slowly approaching. "Yes," continued Jack abruptly, lightly lifting his voice as Mrs. Johnson opened the door, — "yes, if you 'd only had some of those spearmint drops of your aunt Rachel's that she always gave you when these fits came on you 'd have been all right inside of five minutes. Aunty was no slouch of a doctor, was she? Dear me, it only seems yesterday since I saw her. You were just playing round her knee like a kitten on the back porch. How time does fly! But here 's Mrs. Johnson coming to take you in. Now rouse up, Sophy, and just hook yourself on to Mrs. Johnson on that side, and we 'll toddle along."

The young girl put back her heavy hair, and with her face still averted submitted to be helped to her feet by the kindly stewardess. Perhaps something homely sympathetic and nurse-like in the touch of the mulatto gave her assurance and confidence, for her head lapsed quite naturally against the woman's shoulder, and her face was partly hidden as she moved slowly along the deck. Jack accompanied them to the saloon and the inner stateroom door. A few passengers gathered curiously near, as much attracted by the unusual presence of Jack Hamlin in such a procession as by the girl herself. "You 'll look after her specially, Mrs. Johnson," said Jack, in unusually deliberate terms. "She's been a good deal petted at home, and my sister perhaps has rather spoilt her. She's pretty much of a child still, and you'll have to humor her. Sophy," he continued, with ostentatious playfulness, directing his voice to the dim recesses of the stateroom, "you'll just think Mrs. Johnson's your old nurse, won't you? Think it's old Katy, hey?"

To his great consternation the girl approached tremblingly from the inner shadow. The faintest and saddest of smiles for a moment played around the corners of her drawn mouth and tear-dimmed eyes as she held out her hand and said: —

"God bless you for being so kind."

Jack shuddered and glanced quickly round. But luckily no one heard this crushing sentimentalism, and the next moment the door closed upon her and Mrs. Johnson.

It was past midnight, and the moon was riding high over the narrowing yellow river, when Jack again stepped out on deck. He had just left the captain's cabin, and a small social game with the officers, which had served to some extent to vaguely relieve his irritation and their pockets. He had presumably quite forgotten the incident of the afternoon, as he looked about him, and complacently took in the quiet beauty of the night.

The low banks on either side offered no break to the uninterrupted level of the landscape, through which the river seemed to wind only as a race track for the rushing boat. Every fibre of her vast but fragile bulk quivered under the goad of her powerful engines. There was no other movement but hers, no other sound but this monstrous beat and panting; the whole tranquil landscape seemed to breathe and pulsate with her; dwellers in the tules, miles away, heard and felt her as she passed, and it seemed to Jack, leaning over the railing, as if the whole river swept like a sluice through her paddle-boxes.

Jack had quite unconsciously lounged before that part of the railing where the young girl had leaned a few hours ago. As he looked down upon the streaming yellow mill - race below him, he noticed — what neither he nor the girl had probably noticed before — that a space of the top bar of the railing was hinged, and could be lifted by withdrawing a small bolt, thus giving easy access to the guards. He was still looking at it, whistling softly, when footsteps approached.

"Jack," said a lazy voice, "how's sister Mary?"

"It's a long time since you've seen her only child, Jack, ain't it?" said a second voice; "and yet it sort o' seems to me somehow that I've seen her before."

Jack recognized the voice of two of his late companions at the card - table. His whistling ceased ; so also dropped every trace of color and expression from his handsome face. But he did not turn, and remained quietly gazing at the water.

"Aunt Rachel, too, must be getting on in years, Jack," continued the first speaker, halting behind Jack.

"And Mrs. Johnson does not look so much like Sophy's old nurse as she used to," remarked the second, following his example. Still Jack remained unmoved.

"You don't seem to be interested, Jack," continued the first speaker. "What are you looking at?"

Without turning his head the gambler

replied, "Looking at the boat; she's booming along, just chawing up and spitting out the river, ain't she? Look at that sweep of water going under her paddle-wheels," he continued, unbolting the rail and lifting it to allow the two men to peer curiously over the guards as he pointed to the murderous incline beneath them; "a man would n't stand much show who got dropped into it. How these paddles would just snatch him bald-headed, pick him up and slosh him round and round, and then sling him out down there in such a shape that his own father would n't know him."

"Yes," said the first speaker, with an ostentatious little laugh, "but all that ain't telling us how sister Mary is."

"No," said the gambler slipping into the opening with a white and rigid face in which nothing seemed living but the eyes, — "no, but it's telling you how two d—d fools who did n't know when to shut their mouths might get them shut once and forever. It's telling you what might happen to two men who tried to 'play' a man who did n't care to be 'played,' — a man who did n't care much what he did, when he did it, or how he did it, but would do what he 'd set out to do — even if in doing it he went to hell with the men he sent there."

He had stepped out on the guards, beside the two men, closing the rail behind him. He had placed his hands on their shoulders; they had both gripped his arms; yet, viewed from the deck above, they seemed at that moment an amicable, even fraternal group, albeit the faces of the three were dead white in the moonlight.

"I don't think I'm so very much interested in sister Mary," said the first speaker quietly, after a pause.

"And I don't seem to think so much of aunt Rachel as I did," said his companion.

"I thought you would n't," said Jack, coolly reopening the rail and stepping back again. "It all depends upon the way you look at those things. Good-night."

"Good-night."

The three men paused, shook each other's hands silently, and separated, Jack sauntering slowly back to his stateroom.

II.

The educational establishment of Mrs. Mix and Madame Bance, situated in the best quarter of Sacramento and patronized by the highest state officials and members of the clergy, was a pretty if not an imposing edifice. Although surrounded by a high white picket fence and entered through a heavily boarded gate, its balconies festooned with jasmine and roses, and its spotlessly draped windows as often graced with fresh, flower-like faces, were still plainly and provokingly visible above the ostentatious spikes of the pickets. Nevertheless, Mr. Jack Hamlin, who had six months before placed his niece, Miss Sophonisba Brown, under its protecting care, felt a degree of uneasiness, even bordering on timidity, which was new to that usually self-confident man. Remembering how his first appearance had fluttered this dovecote and awakened a severe suspicion in the minds of the two principals, he had discarded his usual fashionable attire and elegantly fitting garments for a rough, homespun suit, supposed to represent a homely agriculturist, but which had the effect of transforming him into an adorable Strephon, infinitely more dangerous in his rustic shepherd-like simplicity. He had also shaved off his silken mustache for the same prudential reasons, but had only succeeded in uncovering the delicate lines of his handsome mouth, and so absurdly reducing his apparent years that his avuncular pretensions seemed more preposterous than ever; and when he had rung the bell and was admitted by a severe Hibernian porteress, his momentary hesitation and half humorous diffidence had such an unexpected effect upon her, that it seemed doubtful if he would be allowed to pass beyond the vestibule. "Shure, miss," she said in a whisper to an under teacher, "there's wan at the dhure who calls himself, 'Mister' Hamlin, but av it is not a young lady maskeradin' in her brother's clothes Oim very much mistaken; and av it's a boy, one of the pupil's brothers, shure ye might put a dhress on him when you take the others out for a walk, and he'd pass for the beauty of the whole school."

Meantime, the unconscious subject of this criticism was pacing somewhat uneasily up and down the formal reception room into which he had been finally ushered. Its farther end was filled by an enormous parlor organ, a number of music books, and a cheerfully variegated globe. A large presentation Bible, an equally massive illustrated volume on the Holy Land, a few landscapes in cold, bluish milk and water colors, and rigid heads in crayons — the work of pupils — were presumably ornamental. An imposing mahogany sofa and what seemed to be a disproportionate excess of chairs somewhat coldly furnished the room. Jack had reluctantly made up his mind that, if Sophy was accompanied by any one, he would be obliged to kiss her to keep up his assumed relationship. As she entered the room with Miss Mix, Jack advanced and soberly saluted her on the cheek. But so positive and apparent was the gallantry of his presence, and perhaps so suggestive of some pastoral flirtation, that Miss Mix, to Jack's surprise, winced perceptibly and became stony. But he was still more surprised that the young lady herself shrank half uneasily from his lips, and uttered a slight exclamation. It was a new experience to Mr. Hamlin.

But this somewhat mollified Miss Mix, and she slightly relaxed her austerity. She was glad to be able to give the best accounts of Miss Brown, not only as regarded her studies, but as to her conduct and deportment. Really, with the present freedom of manners and laxity of home discipline in California, it was gratifying to meet a young lady who seemed to value the importance of a proper decorum and behavior, especially towards the opposite sex. Mr. Hamlin, although her guardian, was perhaps too young to understand and appreciate this. To this experience she must also attribute the indiscretion of his calling during school hours and without preliminary warning. She trusted, however, that this informality could be overlooked after consultation with Madame Bance, but in the mean time, perhaps for half an hour, she must withdraw Miss Brown and return with her to the class. Mr. Hamlin could wait in this public room, reserved especially for visitors, until they returned. Or, if he cared to accompany one of the teachers in a formal inspection of the school, she added, doubtfully, with a glance at Jack's distracting attractions, she would submit this also to Madame Bance.

"Thank you, thank you," returned Jack hurriedly, as a depressing vision of the fifty or sixty scholars rose before his eyes, "but I'd rather not. I mean, you know, I'd

just as lief stay here *alone.* I would n't
have called anyway, don't you see, only I
had a day off, — and — and — I wanted to
talk with my niece on family matters."
He did not say that he had received a somewhat distressful letter from her asking him
to come; a new instinct made him cautious.

Considerably relieved by Jack's unexpected abstention, which seemed to spare
her pupils the distraction of his graces,
Miss Mix smiled more amicably and retired
with her charge. In the single glance he
had exchanged with Sophy he saw that,
although resigned and apparently self-con-
trolled, she still appeared thoughtful and
melancholy. She had improved in appearance and seemed more refined and less rustic in her school dress, but he was conscious
of the same distinct separation of her per-
sonality (which was uninteresting to him)
from the sentiment that had impelled him
to visit her. She was possibly still han-
kering after that fellow Stratton, in spite of
her protestations to the contrary; perhaps
she wanted to go back to her sister, although she had declared she would die first,
and had always refused to disclose her real
name or give any clue by which he could

have traced her relations. She would cry, of course; he almost hoped that she would not return alone; he half regretted he had come. She still held him only by a single quality of her nature, — the desperation she had shown in the boat; that was something he understood and respected.

He walked discontentedly to the window and looked out; he walked discontentedly to the end of the room and stopped before the organ. It was a fine instrument; he could see that with an admiring and experienced eye. He was alone in the room; in fact, quite alone in that part of the house which was separated from the class-rooms. He would disturb no one by trying it. And if he did, what then? He smiled a little recklessly, slowly pulled off his gloves, and sat down before it.

He played cautiously at first, with the soft pedal down. The instrument had never known a strong masculine hand before, having been fumbled and friveled over by softly incompetent, feminine fingers. But presently it began to thrill under the passionate hand of its lover, and carried away by his one innocent weakness, Jack was launched upon a sea of musical reminiscences.   Scraps of church music, Puritan psalms of his boyhood; dying strains from sad, forgotten operas, fragments of oratorios and symphonies, but chiefly phrases from old masses heard at the missions of San Pedro and Santa Isabel, swelled up from his loving and masterful fingers.   He had finished an Agnus Dei; the formal room was pulsating with divine aspirations; the rascal's hands were resting listlessly on the keys, his brown lashes lifted, in an effort of memory, tenderly towards the ceiling.

Suddenly, a subdued murmur of applause and a slight rustle behind him recalled him to himself again.   He wheeled his chair quickly round.   The two principals of the school and half a dozen teachers were standing gravely behind him, and at the open door a dozen curled and frizzled youthful heads peered in eagerly, but half restrained by their teachers.   The relaxed features and apologetic attitude of Madame Bance and Miss Mix showed that Mr. Hamlin had unconsciously achieved a triumph.

He might not have been as pleased to know that his extraordinary performance had solved a difficulty, effaced his other graces, and enabled them to place him on the moral pedestal of a mere musician, to whom these eccentricities were allowable and privileged. He shared the admiration extended by the young ladies to their music teacher, which was always understood to be a sexless enthusiasm and a contagious juvenile disorder. It was also a fine advertisement for the organ. Madame Bance smiled blandly, improved the occasion by thanking Mr. Hamlin for having given the scholars a gratuitous lesson on the capabilities of the instrument, and was glad to be able to give Miss Brown a half-holiday to spend with her accomplished relative. Miss Brown was even now upstairs, putting on her hat and mantle. Jack was relieved. Sophy would not attempt to cry on the street.

Nevertheless, when they reached it and the gate closed behind them, he again became uneasy. The girl's clouded face and melancholy manner were not promising. It also occurred to him that he might meet some one who knew him and thus compromise her. This was to be avoided at all hazards. He began with forced gayety: —

"Well, now, where shall we go?"

She slightly raised her tear-dimmed eyes. "Where you please — I don't care."

"There is n't any show going on here, is there?" He had a vague idea of a circus or menagerie — himself in the shadow of the box behind her.

"I don't know of any."

"Or any restaurant — or cake shop?"

"There 's a place where the girls go to get candy on Main Street. Some of them are there now."

Jack shuddered; this was not to be thought of. "But where do you walk?"

"Up and down Main Street."

"Where everybody can see you?" said Jack, scandalized.

The girl nodded.

They walked on in silence for a few moments. Then a bright idea struck Mr. Hamlin. He suddenly remembered that in one of his many fits of impulsive generosity and largesse he had given to an old negro retainer — whose wife had nursed him through a dangerous illness — a house and lot on the river bank. He had been told that they had opened a small laundry or wash-house. It occurred to him that a stroll there and a call upon "Uncle Hannibal and Aunt Chloe" combined the propriety and respectability due to the young

person he was with, and the requisite se-
crecy and absence of publicity due to himself.   He at once suggested it.

"You see she was a mighty good woman
and you ought to know her, for she was my
old nurse" —

The girl glanced at him with a sudden
impatience.

" Honest Injin," said Jack solemnly ;
"she did nurse me through my last cough.
I ain't playing old family gags on you
now."   ·

"Oh, dear," burst out the girl impulsively, "I do wish you would n't ever play
them again.   I wish you would n't pre-
tend to be my uncle; I wish you would n't
make me pass for your niece.   It is n't
right.   It's all wrong.   Oh, don't you know
it's all wrong, and can't come right any
way?   It's just killing me.   I can't stand
it.   I'd rather you'd say what I am and
how I came to you and how you pitied me."

They had luckily entered a narrow side
street, and the sobs which shook the young
girl's frame were unnoticed.   For a few
moments Jack felt a horrible conviction
stealing over him, that in his present attitude towards her he was not unlike that

hound Stratton, and that, however innocent his own intent, there was a sickening resemblance to the situation on the boat in the base advantage he had taken of her friendlessness. He had never told her that he was a gambler like Stratton, and that his peculiarly infelix reputation among women made it impossible for him to assist her, except by a stealth or the deception he had practiced, without compromising her. He who had for years faced the sneers and half-frightened opposition of the world dared not tell the truth to this girl, from whom he expected nothing and who did not interest him. He felt he was almost slinking at her side. At last he said desperately : —

"But I snatched them bald-headed at the organ, Sophy, did n't I ?"

"Oh yes," said the girl, "you played beautifully and grandly. It was so good of you, too. For I think, somehow, Madame Bance had been a little suspicious of you, but that settled it. Everybody thought it was fine, and some thought it was your profession. Perhaps," she added timidly, "it is ?"

"I play a good deal, I reckon," said

Jack, with a grim humor which did not, however, amuse him.

"I wish *I* could, and make money by it," said the girl eagerly. Jack winced, but she did not notice it as she went on hurriedly: "That's what I wanted to talk to you about. I want to leave the school and make my own living. Anywhere where people won't know me and where I can be alone and work. I shall die here among these girls — with all their talk of their friends and their — sisters, — and their questions about you."

"Tell 'em to dry up," said Jack indignantly. "Take 'em to the cake shop and load 'em up with candy and ice cream. That'll stop their mouths. You've got money, you got my last remittance, didn't you?" he repeated quickly. "If you didn't, here's" — his hand was already in his pocket when she stopped him with a despairing gesture.

"Yes, yes, I got it all. I haven't touched it. I don't want it. For I can't live on you. Don't you understand, — I want to work. Listen, — I can draw and paint. Madame Bance says I do it well; my drawing-master says I might in time take portraits and get paid for it. And even now I can retouch photographs and make colored miniatures from them. And," she stopped and glanced at Jack half-timidly, "I 've — done some already."

A glow of surprised relief suffused the gambler. Not so much at this astonishing revelation as at the change it seemed to effect in her. Her pale blue eyes, made paler by tears, cleared and brightened under their swollen lids like wiped steel; the lines of her depressed mouth straightened and became firm. Her voice had lost its hopeless monotone.

"There 's a shop in the next street, — a photographer's, — where they have one of mine in their windows," she went on, reassured by Jack's unaffected interest. "It 's only round the corner, if you care to see."

Jack assented; a few paces farther brought them to the corner of a narrow street, where they presently turned into a broader thoroughfare and stopped before the window of a photographer. Sophy pointed to an oval frame, containing a portrait painted on porcelain. Mr. Hamlin was startled. Inexperienced as he was, a certain artistic inclination told him it was good, although it is to be feared he would have been astonished even if it had been worse. The mere fact that this headstrong country girl, who had run away with a cur like Stratton, should be able to do anything else took him by surprise.

"I got ten dollars for that," she said hesitatingly, "and I could have got more for a larger one, but I had to do that in my room, during recreation hours. If I had more time and a place where I could work" — she stopped timidly and looked tentatively at Jack. But he was already indulging in a characteristically reckless idea of coming back after he had left Sophy, buying the miniature at an extravagant price, and ordering half a dozen more at extraordinary figures. Here, however, two passers-by, stopping ostensibly to look in the window, but really attracted by the picturesque spectacle of the handsome young rustic and his schoolgirl companion, gave Jack such a fright that he hurried Sophy away again into the side street. "There's nothing mean about that picture business," he said cheerfully; "it looks like a square kind of game," and relapsed into thoughtful silence.

At which, Sophy, the ice of restraint

broken, again burst into passionate appeal. If she could only go away somewhere — where she saw no one but the people who would buy her work, who knew nothing of her past nor cared to know who were her relations! She would work hard; she knew she could support herself in time. She would keep the name he had given her, — it was not distinctive enough to challenge any inquiry, — but nothing more. She need not assume to be his niece; he would always be her kind friend, to whom she owed everything, even her miserable life. She trusted still to his honor never to seek to know her real name, nor ever to speak to her of that man if he ever met him. It would do no good to her or to them; it might drive her, for she was not yet quite sure of herself, to do that which she had promised him never to do again.

There was no threat, impatience, or acting in her voice, but he recognized the same dull desperation he had once heard in it, and her eyes, which a moment before were quick and mobile, had become fixed and set. He had no idea of trying to penetrate the foolish secret of her name and relations; he had never had the slightest curiosity, but it struck him now that Stratton might at any time force it upon him. The only way that he could prevent it was to let it be known that, for unexpressed reasons, he would shoot Stratton "on sight." This would naturally restrict any verbal communication between them. Jack's ideas of morality were vague, but his convictions on points of honor were singularly direct and positive.

III.

Meantime Hamlin and Sophy were passing the outskirts of the town; the open lots and cleared spaces were giving way to grassy stretches, willow copses, and groups of cottonwood and sycamore; and beyond the level of yellowing tules appeared the fringed and raised banks of the river. Half tropical looking cottages with deep verandas — the homes of early Southern pioneers — took the place of incomplete blocks of modern houses, monotonously alike. In these sylvan surroundings Mr. Hamlin's picturesque rusticity looked less incongruous and more Arcadian; the young girl had lost some of her restraint with her confidences, and lounging together side by side, without the least consciousness of any sentiment in their words or actions, they nevertheless contrived to impress the spectator with the idea that they were a charming pair of pastoral lovers. So strong was this impression that, as they approached Aunt Chloe's laundry, a pretty rose-covered cottage with an enormous whitewashed barn-like extension in the rear, the black proprietress herself, standing at the door, called her husband to come and look at them, and flashed her white teeth in such unqualified commendation and patronage that Mr. Hamlin, withdrawing himself from Sophy's side, instantly charged down upon them.

"If you don't slide the lid back over that grinning box of dominoes of yours and take it inside, I 'll just carry Hannibal off with me," he said in a quick whisper, with a half-wicked, half-mischievous glitter in his brown eyes. "That young lady 's — *a lady* — do you understand? No riffraff friend of mine, but a regular *nun* — a saint — do you hear? So you just stand back and let her take a good look round, and rest herself, until she wants you." "Two black idiots, Miss Brown," he continued cheerfully in a higher voice of explanation, as Sophy approached, "who think because one of 'em used to shave me and the other saved my life they 've got a right to stand at their humble cottage door and frighten horses!"

So great was Mr. Hamlin's ascendency over his former servants that even this ingenious pleasantry was received with every sign of affection and appreciation of the humorist, and of the profound respect for his companion. Aunt Chloe showed them effusively into her parlor, a small but scrupulously neat and sweet-smelling apartment, inordinately furnished with a huge mahogany centre-table and chairs, and the most fragile and meretricious china and glass ornaments on the mantel. But the three jasmine-edged lattice windows opened upon a homely garden of old-fashioned herbs and flowers, and their fragrance filled the room. The cleanest and starchiest of curtains, the most dazzling and whitest of tidies and chair-covers, bespoke the adjacent laundry; indeed, the whole cottage seemed to exhale the odors of lavender soap and freshly ironed linen. Yet the cottage was large for the couple and their assistants. "Dar was two front rooms on de next flo' dat dey never used," explained Aunt Chloe; "friends allowed dat dey could let 'em to white folks, but dey had always been done kep' for Marse Hamlin, ef he ever wanted to be wid his old niggers again." Jack looked up quickly with a brightened face, made a sign to Hannibal, and the two left the room together.

When he came through the passage a few moments later, there was a sound of laughter in the parlor. He recognized the full, round lazy chuckle of Aunt Chloe, but there was a higher girlish ripple that he did not know. He had never heard Sophy laugh before. Nor, when he entered, had he ever seen her so animated. She was helping Chloe set the table, to that lady's intense delight at "Missy's" girlish house-wifery. She was picking the berries fresh from the garden, buttering the Sally Lunn, making the tea, and arranging the details of the repast with apparently no trace of her former discontent and unhappiness in either face or manner. He dropped quietly into a chair by the window, and, with the homely scents of the garden mixing with the honest odors of Aunt Chloe's cookery, watched her with an amusement that was as pleasant and grateful as it was strange and unprecedented.

"Now den," said Aunt Chloe to her husband, as she put the finishing touch to the repast in a plate of doughnuts as exquisitely brown and shining as Jack's eyes were at that moment, "Hannibal, you just come away, and let dem two white quality chillens have dey tea. Dey 's done starved, shuah." And with an approving nod to Jack, she bundled her husband from the room.

The door closed; the young girl began to pour out the tea, but Jack remained in his seat by the window. It was a singular sensation which he did not care to disturb. It was no new thing for Mr. Hamlin to find himself at a *tête-à-tête* repast with the admiring and complaisant fair; there was a *cabinet particulier* in a certain San Francisco restaurant which had listened to their various vanities and professions of undying faith; he might have recalled certain festal rendezvous with a widow whose piety and impeccable reputation made it a moral duty for her to come to him only in disguise; it was but a few days before that he had been let privately into the palatial mansion of a high official for a midnight supper with a foolish wife. It was not strange, therefore, that he should be alone here, secretly with a member of that indirect, loving sex. But that he should be sitting there in a cheap negro laundry with absolutely no sentiment of any kind towards the heavy‑haired, freckle‑faced country schoolgirl opposite him, from whom he sought and expected nothing, and *enjoying* it without scorn of himself or his companion, to use his own expression, "got him." Presently he rose and sauntered to the table with shining eyes.

"Well, what do you think of Aunt Chloe's shebang?" he asked smilingly.

"Oh, it's so sweet and clean and homelike," said the girl quickly. At any other time he would have winced at the last adjective. It struck him now as exactly the word.

"Would you like to live here, if you could?"

Her face brightened. She put the teapot down and gazed fixedly at Jack.

"Because you can. Look here. I spoke to Hannibal about it. You can have the two front rooms if you want to. One of 'em is big enough and light enough for a studio to do your work in. You tell that nigger what you want to put in 'em, and he 's got my orders to do it. I told him about your painting; said you were the daughter of an old friend, you know. Hold on, Sophy; d—n it all, I 've got to do a little gilt-edged lying; but I let you out of the niece business this time. Yes, from this moment I 'm no longer your uncle. I renounce the relationship. It 's hard," continued the rascal, "after all these years and considering sister Mary's feelings; but, as you seem to wish it, it must be done."

Sophy's steel-blue eyes softened. She slid her long brown hand across the table and grasped Jack's. He returned the pressure quickly and fraternally, even to that half-shamed, half-hurried evasion of emotion peculiar to all brothers. This was also a new sensation; but he liked it.

"You are too — too good, Mr. Hamlin," she said quietly.

"Yes," said Jack cheerfully, "that 's what 's the matter with me. It is n't natural, and if I keep it up too long it brings on my cough."

Nevertheless, they were happy in a boy and girl fashion, eating heartily, and, I fear, not always decorously; scrambling somewhat for the strawberries, and smacking their lips over the Sally Lunn. Meantime, it was arranged that Mr. Hamlin should inform Miss Mix that Sophy would leave school at the end of the term, only a few days hence, and then transfer herself to lodgings with some old family servants, where she could more easily pursue her studies in her own profession. She need not make her place of abode a secret, neither need she court publicity. She would write to Jack regularly, informing him of her progress, and he would visit her whenever he could. Jack assented gravely to the further proposition that he was to keep a strict account of all the moneys he advanced her, and that she was to repay him out of the proceeds of her first pictures. He had promised also, with a slight mental reservation, not to buy them all himself, but to trust to her success with the public. They were never to talk of what had happened before; she was to begin life anew. Of such were their confidences, spoken often together at the same moment, and with their mouths full. Only one thing troubled Jack; he had not yet told her frankly who he was and what was his reputation; he had hitherto carelessly supposed she would learn it, and in truth had cared little if she did; but it was evident from her conversation that day that by some miracle she was still in ignorance. Unable to tell her himself, he had charged Hannibal to break it to her casually after he was gone. "You can let me down easy if you like, but you'd better make a square deal of it while you're about it. And," Jack had added cheerfully, "if she thinks after that she'd better drop me entirely, you just say that if she wishes to *stay*, you'll see that I don't ever come here again. And you keep your word about it too, you black nigger, or I'll be the first to thrash you."

Nevertheless, when Hannibal and Aunt Chloe returned to clear away the repast, they were a harmonious party; albeit, Mr. Hamlin seemed more content to watch them silently from his chair by the window, a cigar between his lips, and the pleasant distraction of the homely scents and sounds of the garden in his senses. Allusion having been made again to the morning perform-

ance of the organ, he was implored by
Hannibal to diversify his talent by exercis-
ing it on an old guitar which had passed
into that retainer's possession with certain
clothes of his master's when they separated.
Mr. Hamlin accepted it dubiously; it had
twanged under his volatile fingers in more
pretentious but less innocent halls. But
presently he raised his tenor voice and soft
brown lashes to the humble ceiling and
sang.

" Way down upon the Swanee River,"

Discoursed Jack plaintively,—

> " Far, far away,
> Thar's whar my heart is turning ever,
> Thar's whar the old folks stay."

The two dusky scions of an emotional
race, that had been wont to sweeten its toil
and condone its wrongs with music, sat
wrapt and silent, swaying with Jack's voice
until they could burst in upon the chorus.
The jasmine vines trilled softly with the
afternoon breeze; a slender yellow-hammer,
perhaps, emulous of Jack, swung himself
from an outer spray and peered curiously
into the room; and a few neighbors, gathering at their doors and windows, remarked
that "after all, when it came to real sing-

ing, no one could beat those d—d niggers."

The sun was slowly sinking in the rolling
gold of the river when Jack and Sophy
started leisurely back through the broken
shafts of light, and across the far-stretching
shadows of the cottonwoods. In the midst
of a lazy silence they were presently conscious of a distant monotonous throb, the
booming of the up boat on the river. The
sound came nearer — passed them, the boat
itself hidden by the trees; but a trailing
cloud of smoke above cast a momentary
shadow upon their path. The girl looked
up at Jack with a troubled face. Mr.
Hamlin smiled reassuringly; but in that
instant he had made up his mind that it was
his moral duty to kill Mr. Edward Stratton.

IV.

For the next two months Mr. Hamlin
was professionally engaged in San Francisco and Marysville, and the transfer of
Sophy from the school to her new home
was effected without his supervision. From
letters received by him during that interval,
it seemed that the young girl had entered

energetically upon her new career, and that her artistic efforts were crowned with success. There were a few Indian-ink sketches, studies made at school and expanded in her own "studio," which were eagerly bought as soon as exhibited in the photographer's window, — notably by a florid and inartistic bookkeeper, an old negro woman, a slangy stable boy, a gorgeously dressed and painted female, and the bearded second officer of a river steamboat, without hesitation and without comment. This, as Mr. Hamlin intelligently pointed out in a letter to Sophy, showed a general and diversified appreciation on the part of the public. Indeed, it emboldened her, in the retouching of photographs, to offer sittings to the subjects, and to undertake even large crayon copies, which had resulted in her getting so many orders that she was no longer obliged to sell her drawings, but restricted herself solely to profitable portraiture. The studio became known; even its quaint surroundings added to the popular interest, and the originality and independence of the young painter helped her to a genuine success. All this she wrote to Jack. Meantime Hannibal had assured him that he had carried out his instructions by informing "Missy" of his old master's real occupation and reputation, but that the young lady hadn't "took no notice." Certainly there was no allusion to it in her letters, nor any indication in her manner. Mr. Hamlin was greatly, and it seemed to him properly, relieved. And he looked forward with considerable satisfaction to an early visit to old Hannibal's laundry.

It must be confessed, also, that another matter, a simple affair of gallantry, was giving him an equally unusual, unexpected, and absurd annoyance, which he had never before permitted to such trivialities. In a recent visit to a fashionable watering-place, he had attracted the attention of what appeared to be a respectable, matter of fact woman, the wife of a recently elected rural Senator. She was, however, singularly beautiful, and as singularly cold. It was perhaps this quality, and her evident annoyance at some unreasoning prepossession which Jack's fascinations exercised upon her, that heightened that reckless desire for risk and excitement which really made up the greater part of his gallantry. Nevertheless, as was his habit, he had treated her always with a charming unconsciousness of his own attentions, and a frankness that seemed inconsistent with any insidious approach. In fact, Mr. Hamlin seldom made love to anybody, but permitted it to be made to him with good-humored deprecation and cheerful skepticism. He had once, quite accidentally, while riding, come upon her when she had strayed from her own riding party, and had behaved with such unexpected circumspection and propriety, not to mention a certain thoughtful abstraction, — it was the day he had received Sophy's letter, — that she was constrained to make the first advances. This led to a later innocent rendezvous, in which Mrs. Camperly was impelled to confide to Mr. Hamlin the fact that her husband had really never understood her. Jack listened with an understanding and sympathy quickened by long experience of such confessions. If anything had ever kept him from marriage it was this evident incompatibility of the conjugal relations with a just conception of the feminine soul and its aspirations.

And so eventually this yearning for sympathy dragged Mrs. Camperly's clean skirts and rustic purity after Jack's heels into various places and various situations not so clean, rural, or innocent; made her miserably unhappy in his absence, and still more miserably happy in his presence; impelled her to lie, cheat, and bear false witness; forced her to listen with mingled shame and admiration to narrow criticism of his faults, from natures so palpably inferior to his own that her moral sense was confused and shaken; gave her two distinct lives, but so unreal and feverish that, with a recklessness equal to his own, she was at last ready to merge them both into his. For the first time in his life Mr. Hamlin found himself bored at the beginning of an affair, actually hesitated, and suddenly disappeared from San Francisco.

He turned up a few days later at Aunt Chloe's door, with various packages of presents and quite the air of a returning father of a family, to the intense delight of that lady and to Sophy's proud gratification. For he was lost in a profuse, boyish admiration of her pretty studio, and of wholesome reverence for her art and her astounding progress. They were also amused at his awe and evident alarm at the portraits of two ladies, her latest sitters, that were

still on the easels, and, in consideration of
his half-assumed, half-real bashfulness, they
turned their faces to the wall. Then his
quick, observant eye detected a photograph
of himself on the mantel.

"What's that?" he asked suddenly.

Sophy and Aunt Chloe exchanged meaning glances. Sophy had, as a surprise to
Jack, just completed a handsome crayon
portrait of himself from an old photograph
furnished by Hannibal, and the picture was
at that moment in the window of her former
patron, — the photographer.

"Oh, dat! Miss Sophy jus' put it dar fo'
de lady sitters to look at to gib 'em a pleasant
'spresshion," said Aunt Chloe, chuckling.

Mr. Hamlin did not laugh, but quietly
slipped the photograph into his pocket.
Yet, perhaps, it had not been recognized.

Then Sophy proposed to have luncheon
in the studio; it was quite "Bohemian" and
fashionable, and many artists did it. But
to her great surprise Jack gravely objected,
preferring the little parlor of Aunt Chloe,
the vine-fringed windows, and the heavy
respectable furniture. He thought it was
profaning the studio, and then — anybody
might come in. This unusual circumspec-

tion amused them, and was believed to be part of the boyish awe with which Jack regarded the models, the draperies, and the studies on the walls. Certain it was that he was much more at his ease in the parlor, and when he and Sophy were once more alone at their meal, although he ate nothing, he had regained all his old naïveté. Presently he leaned forward and placed his hand fraternally on her arm. Sophy looked up with an equally frank smile.

"You know I promised to let bygones be bygones, eh? Well, I intended it, and more, — I intended to make 'em so. I told you I'd never speak to you again of that man who tried to run you off, and I intended that no one else should. Well, as he was the only one who could talk — that meant him. But the cards are out of my hands; the game's been played without me. For he's dead!"

The girl started. Mr. Hamlin's hand passed caressingly twice or thrice along her sleeve with a peculiar gentleness that seemed to magnetize her.

"Dead," he repeated slowly. "Shot in San Diego by another man, but not by me. I had him tracked as far as that, and had my eyes on him, but it was n't my deal. But there," he added, giving her magnetized arm a gentle and final tap as if to awaken it, "he 's dead, and so is the whole story.   And now we 'll drop it forever."

The girl's downcast eyes were fixed on the table.   "But there 's my sister," she murmured.

"Did she know you went with him?" asked Jack.

"No; but she knows I ran away."

"Well, you ran away from home to study how to be an artist, don't you see?   Some day she 'll find out you *are one ;* that settles the whole thing."

They were both quite cheerful again when Aunt Chloe returned to clear the table, especially Jack, who was in the best spirits, with preternaturally bright eyes and a somewhat rare color on his cheeks.   Aunt Chloe, who had noticed that his breathing was hurried at times, watched him narrowly, and when later he slipped from the room, followed him into the passage.   He was leaning against the wall.   In an instant the negress was at his side.

"De Lawdy Gawd, Marse Jack, not *agin ?*"

He took his handkerchief, slightly streaked with blood, from his lips and said faintly, "Yes, it came on — on the boat; but I thought the d—d thing was over. Get me out of this, quick, to some hotel, before she knows it. You can tell her I was called away. Say that " — but his breath failed him, and when Aunt Chloe caught him like a child in her strong arms he could make no resistance.

In another hour he was unconscious, with two doctors at his bedside, in the little room that had been occupied by Sophy. It was a sharp attack, but prompt attendance and skillful nursing availed; he rallied the next day, but it would be weeks, the doctors said, before he could be removed in safety. Sophy was transferred to the parlor, but spent most of her time at Jack's bedside with Aunt Chloe, or in the studio with the door open between it and the bedroom. In spite of his enforced idleness and weakness, it was again a singularly pleasant experience to Jack; it amused him to sometimes see Sophy at her work through the open door, and when sitters came, — for he had insisted on her continuing her duties as before, keeping his invalid presence in the house a secret, — he had all the satisfaction of a mischievous boy in rehearsing to Sophy such of the conversation as could be overheard through the closed door, and speculating on the possible wonder and chagrin of the sitters had they discovered him. Even when he was convalescent and strong enough to be helped into the parlor and garden, he preferred to remain propped up in Sophy's little bedroom. It was evident, however, that this predilection was connected with no suggestion nor reminiscence of Sophy herself. It was true that he had once asked her if it did n't make her "feel like home." The decided negative from Sophy seemed to mildly surprise him. "That 's odd," he said; "now all these fixings and things," pointing to the flowers in a vase, the little hanging shelf of books, the knickknacks on the mantel-shelf, and the few feminine ornaments that still remained, "look rather like home to me."

So the days slipped by, and although Mr. Hamlin was soon able to walk short distances, leaning on Sophy's arm, in the evening twilight, along the river bank, he was still missed from the haunts of dissipated men. A good many people won-

dered, and others, chiefly of the more ir-
repressible sex, were singularly concerned.
Apparently one of these, one sultry afternoon, stopped before the shadowed window
of a photographer's; she was a handsome,
well-dressed woman, yet bearing a certain
countrylike simplicity that was unlike the
restless smartness of the more urban prom-
enaders that passed her.   Nevertheless she
had halted before Mr. Hamlin's picture,
which Sophy had not yet dared to bring
home and present to him, and was gazing
at it with rapt and breathless attention.
Suddenly she shook down her veil and entered the shop.   Could the proprietor kindly
tell her if that portrait was the work of a
local artist?

The proprietor was both proud and
pleased to say that *it was!*   It was the
work of a Miss Brown, a young girl student; in fact, a mere schoolgirl one might
say.   He could show her others of her pictures.

Thanks.   But could he tell her if this
portrait was from life?

No doubt; the young lady had a studio,
and he himself had sent her sitters.

And perhaps this was the portrait of one
that he had sent her?

No; but she was very popular and becoming quite the fashion. Very probably this gentleman, whom he understood was quite a public character, had heard of her, and selected her on that account.

The lady's face flushed slightly. The photographer continued. The picture was not for sale; it was only there on exhibition; in fact it was to be returned to-morrow.

To the sitter?

He couldn't say. It was to go back to the studio. Perhaps the sitter would be there.

And this studio? Could she have its address?

The man wrote a few lines on his card. Perhaps the lady would be kind enough to say that he had sent her. The lady, thanking him, partly lifted her veil to show a charming smile, and gracefully withdrew. The photographer was pleased. Miss Brown had evidently got another sitter, and, from that momentary glimpse of her face, it would be a picture as beautiful and attractive as the man's. But what was the odd idea that struck him? She certainly reminded him of some one! There was the same heavy hair, only this lady's was golden, and she was older and more mature. And he remained for a moment with knitted brows musing over his counter.

Meantime the fair stranger was making her way towards the river suburb. When she reached Aunt Chloe's cottage, she paused, with the unfamiliar curiosity of a newcomer, over its quaint and incongruous exterior. She hesitated a moment also when Aunt Chloe appeared in the doorway, and, with a puzzled survey of her features, went upstairs to announce a visitor. There was the sound of hurried shutting of doors, of the moving of furniture, quick footsteps across the floor, and then a girlish laugh that startled her. She ascended the stairs breathlessly to Aunt Chloe's summons, found the negress on the landing, and knocked at a door which bore a card marked "Studio." The door opened; she entered; there were two sudden outcries that might have come from one voice.

"Sophonisba!"

"Marianne!"

"Hush."

The woman had seized Sophy by the wrist and dragged her to the window.

There was a haggard look of desperation in her face akin to that which Hamlin had once seen in her sister's eyes on the boat, as she said huskily: "I did not know *you* were here. I came to see the woman who had painted Mr. Hamlin's portrait. I did not know it was *you.* Listen! Quick! answer me one question. Tell me — I implore you — for the sake of the mother who bore us both! — tell me — is this the man for whom you left home?"

"No! No! A hundred times no!"

Then there was a silence. Mr. Hamlin from the bedroom heard no more.

An hour later, when the two women opened the studio door, pale but composed, they were met by the anxious and tearful face of Aunt Chloe.

"Lawdy Gawd, Missy, — but dey done gone! — bofe of 'em!"

"Who is gone?" demanded Sophy, as the woman beside her trembled and grew paler still.

"Marse Jack and dat fool nigger, Hannibal."

"Mr. Hamlin gone?" repeated Sophy incredulously. "When? Where?"

"Jess now — on de down boat. Sudden

business.   Did n't like to disturb yo' and yo' friend.   Said he 'd write."

" But he was ill — almost helpless," gasped Sophy.

"Dat 's why he took dat old nigger. Lawdy, Missy, bress yo' heart. Dey both knows aich udder, shuah! It 's all right. Dar now, dar dey are; listen."

She held up her hand.   A slow pulsation, that might have been the dull, labored beating of their own hearts, was making itself felt throughout the little cottage.   It came nearer, — a deep regular inspiration that seemed slowly to fill and possess the whole tranquil summer twilight.   It was nearer still — was abreast of the house — passed — grew fainter and at last died away like a deep-drawn sigh.   It was the down boat, that was now separating Mr. Hamlin and his protégée, even as it had once brought them together.

AN INGÉNUE OF THE SIERRAS.

I.

WE all held our breath as the coach rushed through the semi-darkness of Galloper's Ridge. The vehicle itself was only a huge lumbering shadow; its side-lights were carefully extinguished, and Yuba Bill had just politely removed from the lips of an outside passenger even the cigar with which he had been ostentatiously exhibiting his coolness. For it had been rumored that the Ramon Martinez gang of "road agents" were "laying" for us on the second grade, and would time the passage of our lights across Galloper's in order to intercept us in the "brush" beyond. If we could cross the ridge without being seen, and so get through the brush before they reached it, we were safe. If they followed, it would only be a stern chase with the odds in our favor.

The huge vehicle swayed from side to side, rolled, dipped, and plunged, but Bill kept the track, as if, in the whispered words of the Expressman, he could "feel and smell" the road he could no longer see. We knew that at times we hung perilously over the edge of slopes that eventually dropped a thousand feet sheer to the tops of the sugar-pines below, but we knew that Bill knew it also. The half visible heads of the horses, drawn wedge-wise together by the tightened reins, appeared to cleave the darkness like a ploughshare, held between his rigid hands. Even the hoof-beats of the six horses had fallen into a vague, monotonous, distant roll. Then the ridge was crossed, and we plunged into the still blacker obscurity of the brush. Rather we no longer seemed to move — it was only the phantom night that rushed by us. The horses might have been submerged in some swift Lethean stream; nothing but the top of the coach and the rigid bulk of Yuba Bill arose above them. Yet even in that awful moment our speed was unslackened; it was as if Bill cared no longer to *guide* but only to drive, or as if the direction of his huge machine was determined by other hands than his. An incautious whisperer hazarded the paralyzing

suggestion of our "meeting another team."
To our great astonishment Bill overheard
it; to our greater astonishment he replied.
"It 'ud be only a neck and neck race which
would get to h—ll first," he said quietly.
But we were relieved — for he had *spoken!*
Almost simultaneously the wider turnpike
began to glimmer faintly as a visible track
before us; the wayside trees fell out of line,
opened up, and dropped off one after another; we were on the broader table-land,
out of danger, and apparently unperceived
and unpursued.

Nevertheless in the conversation that
broke out again with the relighting of the
lamps, and the comments, congratulations,
and reminiscences that were freely exchanged, Yuba Bill preserved a dissatisfied
and even resentful silence. The most gen-
erous praise of his skill and courage awoke
no response. "I reckon the old man waz
just spilin' for a fight, and is feelin' disappointed," said a passenger. But those who
knew that Bill had the true fighter's scorn
for any purely purposeless conflict were
more or less concerned and watchful of him.
He would drive steadily for four or five
minutes with thoughtfully knitted brows,

but eyes still keenly observant under his slouched hat, and then, relaxing his strained attitude, would give way to a movement of impatience. "You ain't uneasy about any-thing, Bill, are you?" asked the Express-man confidentially. Bill lifted his eyes with a slightly contemptuous surprise. "Not about anything ter *come*. It's what *hez* happened that I don't exackly *sabe*. I don't see no signs of Ramon's gang ever havin' been out at all, and ef they were out I don't see why they did n't go for us."

"The simple fact is that our ruse was successful," said an outside passenger. "They waited to see our lights on the ridge, and, not seeing them, missed us until we had passed. That's my opinion."

"You ain't puttin' any price on that opinion, air ye?" inquired Bill politely.

"No."

"'Cos thar 's a comic paper in 'Frisco pays for them things, and I 've seen worse things in it."

"Come off, Bill," retorted the passenger, slightly nettled by the tittering of his com-panions. "Then what did you put out the lights for?"

"Well," returned Bill grimly, "it mout

have been because I did n't keer to hev you chaps blazin' away at the first bush you *thought* you saw move in your skeer, and bringin' down their fire on us."

The explanation, though unsatisfactory, was by no means an improbable one, and we thought it better to accept it with a laugh. Bill, however, resumed his abstracted manner.

"Who got in at the Summit?" he at last asked abruptly of the Expressman.

"Derrick and Simpson of Cold Spring, and one of the 'Excelsior' boys," responded the Expressman.

"And that Pike County girl from Dow's Flat, with her bundles. 'Don't forget her," added the outside passenger ironically.

"Does anybody here know her?" continued Bill, ignoring the irony.

"You 'd better ask Judge Thompson; he was mighty attentive to her; gettin' her a seat by the off window, and lookin' after her bundles and things."

"Gettin' her a seat by the *window?*" repeated Bill.

"Yes, she wanted to see everything, and was n't afraid of the shooting."

"Yes," broke in a third passenger, "and

he was so d—d civil that when she dropped
her ring in the straw, he struck a match
agin all your rules, you know, and held it
for her to find it.   And it was just as we
were crossin' through the brush, too.   I saw
the hull thing through the window, for I
was hanging over the wheels with my gun
ready for action.   And it was n't no fault
of Judge Thompson's if his d—d foolishness
had n't shown us up, and got us a shot from
the gang."

Bill gave a short grunt, but drove steadily
on without further comment or even turning
his eyes to the speaker.

We were now not more than a mile from
the station at the crossroads where we were
to change horses.   The lights already glimmered in the distance, and there was a faint
suggestion of the coming dawn on the summits of the ridge to the west.   We had
plunged into a belt of timber, when suddenly a horseman emerged at a sharp canter
from a trail that seemed to be parallel with
our own.   We were all slightly startled;
Yuba Bill alone preserving his moody calm.

"Hullo!" he said.

The stranger wheeled to our side as Bill
slackened his speed.   He seemed to be a
"packer" or freight muleteer.

"Ye did n't get ' held up' on the Divide?" continued Bill cheerfully.

"No," returned the packer, with a laugh; "*I* don't carry treasure. But I see you 're all right, too. I saw you crossin' over Galloper's."

"*Saw* us?" said Bill sharply. "We had our lights out."

"Yes, but there was suthin' white — a handkerchief or woman's veil, I reckon — hangin' from the window. It was only a movin' spot agin the hillside, but ez I was lookin' out for ye I knew it was you by that. Good-night!"

He cantered away. We tried to look at each other's faces, and at Bill's expression in the darkness, but he neither spoke nor stirred until he threw down the reins when we stopped before the station. The passengers quickly descended from the roof; the Expressman was about to follow, but Bill plucked his sleeve.

"I 'm goin' to take a look over this yer stage and these yer passengers with ye, afore we start."

"Why, what 's up?"

"Well," said Bill, slowly disengaging himself from one of his enormous gloves, "when we waltzed down into the brush up there I saw a man, ez plain ez I see you, rise up from it. I thought our time had come and the band was goin' to play, when he sorter drew back, made a sign, and we just scooted past him."

"Well?"

"Well," said Bill, "it means that this yer coach was *passed through free* to-night."

"You don't object to *that* — surely? I think we were deucedly lucky."

Bill slowly drew off his other glove. "I 've been riskin' my everlastin' life on this d——d line three times a week," he said with mock humility, "and I 'm allus thankful for small mercies. *But,*" he added grimly, "when it comes down to being passed free by some pal of a hoss thief, and thet called a speshal Providence, *I ain't in it!* No, sir, I ain't in it!"

II.

It was with mixed emotions that the passengers heard that a delay of fifteen minutes to tighten certain screw-bolts had been ordered by the autocratic Bill. Some were anxious to get their breakfast at Sugar

Pine, but others were not averse to linger for the daylight that promised greater safety on the road. The Expressman, knowing the real cause of Bill's delay, was nevertheless at a loss to understand the object of it. The passengers were all well known; any idea of complicity with the road agents was wild and impossible, and, even if there was a confederate of the gang among them, he would have been more likely to precipitate a robbery than to check it. Again, the discovery of such a confederate — to whom they clearly owed their safety — and his arrest would have been quite against the Californian sense of justice, if not actually illegal. It seemed evident that Bill's quixotic sense of honor was leading him astray.

The station consisted of a stable, a wagon shed, and a building containing three rooms. The first was fitted up with " bunks " or sleeping berths for the employees; the second was the kitchen; and the third and larger apartment was dining-room or sitting-room, and was used as general waiting-room for the passengers. It was not a refreshment station, and there was no "bar." But a mysterious command from the omnipotent Bill produced a demijohn of whiskey, with which he hospitably treated the company. The seductive influence of the liquor loosened the tongue of the gallant Judge Thompson. He admitted to having struck a match to enable the fair Pike Countian to find her ring, which, however, proved to have fallen in her lap. She was "a fine, healthy young woman — a type of the Far West, sir; in fact, quite a prairie blossom! yet simple and guileless as a child." She was on her way to Marysville, he believed, "although she expected to meet friends — a friend, in fact — later on." It was her first visit to a large town — in fact, any civilized centre — since she crossed the plains three years ago. Her girlish curiosity was quite touching, and her innocence irresistible. In fact, in a country whose tendency was to produce "frivolity and forwardness in young girls, he found her a most interesting young person." She was even then out in the stable-yard watching the horses being harnessed, "preferring to indulge a pardonable healthy young curiosity than to listen to the empty compliments of the younger passengers."

The figure which Bill saw thus engaged, without being otherwise distinguished, certainly seemed to justify the Judge's opinion. She appeared to be a well-matured country girl, whose frank gray eyes and large laughing mouth expressed a wholesome and abiding gratification in her life and surroundings. She was watching the replacing of luggage in the boot. A little feminine start, as one of her own parcels was thrown somewhat roughly on the roof, gave Bill his opportunity. "Now there," he growled to the helper, "ye ain't carting stone! Look out, will yer! Some of your things, miss?" he added, with gruff courtesy, turning to her. "These yer trunks, for instance?"

She smiled a pleasant assent, and Bill, pushing aside the helper, seized a large square trunk in his arms. But from excess of zeal, or some other mischance, his foot slipped, and he came down heavily, striking the corner of the trunk on the ground and loosening its hinges and fastenings. It was a cheap, common-looking affair, but the accident discovered in its yawning lid a quantity of white, lace-edged feminine apparel of an apparently superior quality. The young lady uttered another cry and came quickly forward, but Bill was profuse in his apologies, himself girded the broken box with a strap, and declared his intention of having the company "make it good " to her with a new one. Then he casually accompanied her to the door of the waiting-room, entered, made a place for her before the fire by simply lifting the nearest and most youthful passenger by the coat collar from the stool that he was occupying, and, having installed the lady in it, displaced another man who was standing before the chimney, and, drawing himself up to his full six feet of height in front of her, glanced down upon his fair passenger as he took his waybill from his pocket.

"Your name is down here as Miss Mullins? " he said.

She looked up, became suddenly aware that she and her questioner were the centre of interest to the whole circle of passengers, and, with a slight rise of color, returned, "Yes."

"Well, Miss Mullins, I 've got a question or two to ask ye. I ask it straight out afore this crowd. It 's in my rights to take ye aside and ask it — but that ain't my style; I 'm no detective. I need n't ask it at all, but act as ef I knowed the answer, or I

might leave it to be asked by others.   Ye
need n't answer it ef ye don't like; ye 've
got a friend over ther — Judge Thompson
— who is a friend to ye, right or wrong,
jest as any other man here is — as though
ye 'd packed your own jury.   Well, the
simple question I 've got to ask ye is *this:*
Did you signal to anybody from the coach
when we passed Galloper's an hour ago?"

We all thought that Bill's courage and
audacity had reached its climax here.   To
openly and publicly accuse a "lady" before
a group of chivalrous Californians, and
that lady possessing the further attractions
of youth, good looks, and innocence, was
little short of desperation.   There was an
evident movement of adhesion towards the
fair stranger, a slight muttering broke out
on the right, but the very boldness of the
act held them in stupefied surprise.   Judge
Thompson, with a bland propitiatory smile
began: "Really, Bill, I must protest on
behalf of this young lady " — when the fair
accused, raising her eyes to her accuser, to
the consternation of everybody answered
with the slight but convincing hesitation of
conscientious truthfulness: —

"*I did.*"

"Ahem!" interposed the Judge hastily, "er — that is — er — you allowed your handkerchief to flutter from the window, — I noticed it myself, — casually — one might say even playfully — but without any particular significance."

The girl, regarding her apologist with a singular mingling of pride and impatience, returned briefly: —.

"I signaled."

"Who did you signal to?" asked Bill gravely.

"The young gentleman I'm going to marry."

A start, followed by a slight titter from the younger passengers, was instantly suppressed by a savage glance from Bill.

"What did you signal to him for?" he continued.

"To tell him I was here, and that it was all right," returned the young girl, with a steadily rising pride and color.

"Wot was all right?" demanded Bill.

"That I was n't followed, and that he could meet me on the road beyond Cass's Ridge Station." She hesitated a moment, and then, with a still greater pride, in which a youthful defiance was still mingled, said:

"I 've run away from home to marry him. And I mean to! No one can stop me. Dad did n't like him just because he was poor, and dad 's got money. Dad wanted me to marry a man I hate, and got a lot of dresses and things to bribe me."

"And you 're taking them in your trunk to the other feller?" said Bill grimly.

"Yes, he 's poor," returned the girl defiantly.

"Then your father's name is Mullins?" asked Bill.

"It 's not Mullins. I — I — took that name," she hesitated, with her first exhibition of self-consciousness.

"Wot *is* his name?"

"Eli Hemmings."

A smile of relief and significance went round the circle. The fame of Eli or "Skinner" Hemmings, as a notorious miser and usurer, had passed even beyond Galloper's Ridge.

"The step that you 're taking, Miss Mullins, I need not tell you, is one of great gravity," said Judge Thompson, with a certain paternal seriousness of manner, in which, however, we were glad to detect a glaring affectation; "and I trust that you

and your affianced have fully weighed it.
Far be it from me to interfere with or question the natural affections of two young
people, but may I ask you what you know
of the — er — young gentleman for whom
you are sacrificing so much, and, perhaps,
imperiling your whole future? For instance, have you known him long?"

The slightly troubled air of trying to
understand, — not unlike the vague won-
derment of childhood, — with which Miss
Mullins had received the beginning of this
exordium, changed to a relieved smile of
comprehension as she said quickly, "Oh
yes, nearly a whole year."

"And," said the Judge, smiling, "has he
a vocation — is he in business?"

"Oh yes," she returned; "he's a collector."

"A collector?"

"Yes; he collects bills, you know, —
money," she went on, with childish eager-
ness, "not for himself, — *he* never has any
money, poor Charley, — but for his firm.
It's dreadful hard work, too; keeps him
out for days and nights, over bad roads and
baddest weather. Sometimes, when he's
stole over to the ranch just to see me, he's

been so bad he could scarcely keep his seat in the saddle, much less stand. And he's got to take mighty big risks, too. Times the folks are cross with him and won't pay; once they shot him in the arm, and he came to me, and I helped do it up for him. But he don't mind. He's real brave, — jest as brave as he's good." There was such a wholesome ring of truth in this pretty praise that we were touched in sympathy with the speaker.

"What firm does he collect for?" asked the Judge gently.

"I don't know exactly — he won't tell me; but I think it's a Spanish firm. You see" — she took us all into her confidence with a sweeping smile of innocent yet half-mischievous artfulness — "I only know because I peeped over a letter he once got from his firm, telling him he must hustle up and be ready for the road the next day; but I think the name was Martinez — yes, Ramon Martinez."

In the dead silence that ensued — a silence so profound that we could hear the horses in the distant stable-yard rattling their harness — one of the younger "Excelsior" boys burst into a hysteric laugh, but the fierce eye of Yuba Bill was down upon him, and seemed to instantly stiffen him into a silent, grinning mask. The young girl, however, took no note of it. Following out, with lover-like diffusiveness, the reminiscences thus awakened, she went on: —

"Yes, it's mighty hard work, but he says it's all for me, and as soon as we're married he'll quit it. He might have quit it before, but he won't take no money of me, nor what I told him I could get out of dad! That ain't his style. He's mighty proud — if he is poor — is Charley. Why thar's all ma's money which she left me in the Savin's Bank that I wanted to draw out — for I had the right — and give it to him, but he wouldn't hear of it! Why, he wouldn't take one of the things I've got with me, if he knew it. And so he goes on ridin' and ridin', here and there and everywhere, and gettin' more and more played out and sad, and thin and pale as a spirit, and always so uneasy about his business, and startin' up at times when we're meetin' out in the South Woods or in the far clearin', and sayin': 'I must be goin' now, Polly,' and yet always tryin' to be chiffle and chipper afore me. Why he must have rid miles and miles to have watched for me thar in the brush at the foot of Galloper's to-night, jest to see if all was safe; and Lordy! I 'd have given him the signal and showed a light if I 'd died for it the next minit. There! That 's what I know of Charley — that 's what I 'm running away from home for — that 's what I 'm running to him for, and I don't care who knows it! And I only wish I 'd done it afore — and I would — if — if — if — he 'd only *asked me!* There now!" She stopped, panted, and choked. Then one of the sudden transitions of youthful emotion overtook the eager, laughing face; it clouded up with the swift change of childhood, a lightning quiver of expression broke over it, and — then came the rain!

I think this simple act completed our utter demoralization! We smiled feebly at each other with that assumption of masculine superiority which is miserably conscious of its own helplessness at such moments. We looked out of the window, blew our noses, said: "Eh — what?" and "I say," vaguely to each other, and were greatly relieved, and yet apparently astonished, when Yuba Bill, who had turned his back upon

the fair speaker, and was kicking the logs
in the fireplace, suddenly swept down upon
us and bundled us all into the road, leaving
Miss Mullins alone.   Then he walked aside
with Judge Thompson for a few moments;
returned to us, autocratically demanded of
the party a complete reticence towards Miss
Mullins on the subject - matter under dis-
cussion, reëntered the station, reappeared
with the young lady, suppressed a faint
idiotic cheer which broke from us at the
spectacle of her innocent face once more
cleared and rosy, climbed the box, and in
another moment we were under way.

"Then she don't know what her lover is
yet?" asked the Expressman eagerly.

"No."

"Are *you* certain it's one of the gang?"

"Can't say *for sure*.   It mout be a young
chap from Yolo who bucked agin the tiger[1]
at Sacramento, got regularly cleaned out
and busted, and joined the gang for a flier.
They say thar was a new hand in that job
over at Keeley's, — and a mighty game one,
too; and ez there was some buckshot on-
loaded that trip, he might hev got his share,
and that would tally with what the girl said

---

[1] Gambled at faro.

about his arm. See! Ef that's the man, I 've heered he was the son of some big preacher in the States, and a college sharp to boot, who ran wild in 'Frisco, and played himself for all he was worth. They 're the wust kind to kick when they once get a foot over the traces. For stiddy, comf'ble kempany," added Bill reflectively, "give *me* the son of a man that was *hanged!*"

"But what are you going to do about this?"

"That depends upon the feller who comes to meet her."

"But you ain't going to try to take him? That would be playing it pretty low down on them both."

"Keep your hair on, Jimmy! The Judge and me are only going to rastle with the sperrit of that gay young galoot, when he drops down for his girl — and exhort him pow'ful! Ef he allows he 's convicted of sin and will find the Lord, we 'll marry him and the gal offhand at the next station, and the Judge will officiate himself for nothin'. We 're goin' to have this yer elopement done on the square — and our waybill clean — you bet!"

"But you don't suppose he 'll trust himself in your hands?"

"Polly will signal to him that it 's all square."

"Ah!" said the Expressman. Nevertheless in those few moments the men seemed to have exchanged dispositions. The Expressman looked doubtfully, critically, and even cynically before him. Bill's face had relaxed, and something like a bland smile beamed across it, as he drove confidently and unhesitatingly forward.

Day, meantime, although full blown and radiant on the mountain summits around us, was yet nebulous and uncertain in the valleys into which we were plunging. Lights still glimmered in the cabins and few ranch buildings which began to indicate the thicker settlements. And the shadows were heaviest in a little copse, where a note from Judge Thompson in the coach was handed up to Yuba Bill, who at once slowly began to draw up his horses. The coach stopped finally near the junction of a small crossroad. At the same moment Miss Mullins slipped down from the vehicle, and, with a parting wave of her hand to the Judge, who had assisted her from the steps, tripped down the crossroad, and disappeared in its semi-obscurity. To our surprise the stage waited, Bill holding the reins listlessly in his hands. Five minutes passed — an eternity of expectation, and, as there was that in Yuba Bill's face which forbade idle questioning, an aching void of silence also! This was at last broken by a strange voice from the road : —

"Go on — we 'll follow."

The coach started forward. Presently we heard the sound of other wheels behind us. We all craned our necks backward to get a view of the unknown, but by the growing light we could only see that we were followed at a distance by a buggy with two figures in it. Evidently Polly Mullins and her lover! We hoped that they would pass us. But the vehicle, although drawn by a fast horse, preserved its distance always, and it was plain that its driver had no desire to satisfy our curiosity. The Expressman had recourse to Bill.

"Is it the man you thought of?" he asked eagerly.

"I reckon," said Bill briefly.

"But," continued the Expressman, returning to his former skepticism, "what 's to keep them both from levanting together now?"

Bill jerked his hand towards the boot with a grim smile.

"Their baggage."

"Oh!" said the Expressman.

"Yes," continued Bill. "We 'll hang on to that gal's little frills and fixin's until this yer job 's settled, and the ceremony 's over, jest as ef we waz her own father. And, what 's more, young man," he added, suddenly turning to the Expressman, "*you 'll* express them trunks of hers *through to Sacramento* with your kempany's labels, and hand her the receipts and checks for them, so she *can get 'em there.* That 'll keep *him* outer temptation and the reach o' the gang, until they get away among white men and civilization again. When your hoary-headed ole grandfather, or, to speak plainer, that partikler old whiskey-soaker known as Yuba Bill, wot sits on this box," he continued, with a diabolical wink at the Expressman, "waltzes in to pervide for a young couple jest startin' in life, thar 's nothin' mean about his style, you bet. He fills the bill every time! Speshul Providences take a back seat when he 's around."

When the station hotel and straggling settlement of Sugar Pine, now distinct and

clear in the growing light, at last rose
within rifleshot on the plateau, the buggy
suddenly darted swiftly by us, so swiftly
that the faces of the two occupants were
barely distinguishable as they passed, and
keeping the lead by a dozen lengths, reached
the door of the hotel. The young girl and
her companion leaped down and vanished
within as we drew up. They had evidently
determined to elude our curiosity, and were
successful.

But the material appetites of the passengers, sharpened by the keen mountain air,
were more potent than their curiosity, and,
as the breakfast-bell rang out at the moment the stage stopped, a majority of them
rushed into the dining-room and scrambled
for places without giving much heed to
the vanished couple or to the Judge and
Yuba Bill, who had disappeared also. The
through coach to Marysville and Sacramento was likewise waiting, for Sugar Pine
was the limit of Bill's ministration, and the
coach which we had just left went no farther. In the course of twenty minutes,
however, there was a slight and somewhat
ceremonious bustling in the hall and on the
veranda, and Yuba Bill and the Judge re-

appeared. The latter was leading, with some elaboration of manner and detail, the shapely figure of Miss Mullins, and Yuba Bill was accompanying her companion to the buggy. We all rushed to the windows to get a good view of the mysterious stranger and probable ex-brigand whose life was now linked with our fair fellow-passenger. I am afraid, however, that we all participated in a certain impression of disappointment and doubt. Handsome and even cultivated-looking, he assuredly was — young and vigorous in appearance. But there was a certain half-shamed, half-defiant suggestion in his expression, yet coupled with a watchful lurking uneasiness which was not pleasant and hardly becoming in a bridegroom — and the possessor of such a bride. But the frank, joyous, innocent face of Polly Mullins, resplendent with a simple, happy confidence, melted our hearts again, and condoned the fellow's shortcomings. We waved our hands; I think we would have given three rousing cheers as they drove away if the omnipotent eye of Yuba Bill had not been upon us. It was well, for the next moment we were summoned to the presence of that soft-hearted autocrat.

We found him alone with the Judge in a private sitting - room, standing before a table on which there was a decanter and glasses. As we filed expectantly into the room and the door closed behind us, he cast a glance of hesitating tolerance over the group.

"Gentlemen," he said slowly, "you was all present at the beginnin' of a little game this mornin', and the Judge thar thinks that you oughter be let in at the finish. *I* don't see that it's any of *your* d—d business — so to speak; but ez the Judge here allows you're all in the secret, I've called you in to take a partin' drink to the health of Mr. and Mrs. Charley Byng — ez is now comf'ably off on their bridal tower. What *you* know or what *you* suspects of the young galoot that's married the gal ain't worth shucks to anybody, and I wouldn't give it to a yaller pup to play with, but the Judge thinks you ought all to promise right here that you'll keep it dark. That's his opinion. Ez far as my opinion goes, gen'l'men," continued Bill, with greater blandness and apparent cordiality, "I wanter simply remark, in a keerless, offhand gin'ral way, that ef I ketch any God-forsaken, lop-

eared, chuckle-headed blatherin' idjet airin'
his opinion " —

"One moment, Bill," interposed Judge
Thompson with a grave smile ; "let me
explain. You understand, gentlemen," he
said, turning to us, "the singular, and I
may say affecting, situation which our good-
hearted friend here has done so much to
bring to what we hope will be a happy ter-
mination. I want to give here, as my professional opinion, that there is nothing in
his request which, in your capacity as good
citizens and law-abiding men, you may not
grant. I want to tell you, also, that you
are condoning no offense against the stat-
utes; that there is not a particle of legal
evidence before us of the criminal antece-
dents of Mr. Charles Byng, except that
which has been told you by the innocent
lips of his betrothed, which the law of the
land has now sealed forever in the mouth
of his wife, and that our own actual experience of his acts have been in the main ex-
culpatory of any previous irregularity — if
not incompatible with it. Briefly, no judge
would charge, no jury convict, on such evidence. When I add that the young girl is
of legal age, that there is no evidence of

any previous undue influence, but rather of the reverse, on the part of the bridegroom, and that I was content, as a magistrate, to perform the ceremony, I think you will be satisfied to give your promise, for the sake of the bride, and drink a happy life to them both."

I need not say that we did this cheerfully, and even extorted from Bill a grunt of satisfaction. The majority of the company, however, who were going with the through coach to Sacramento, then took their leave, and, as we accompanied them to the veranda, we could see that Miss Polly Mullins's trunks were already transferred to the other vehicle under the protecting seals and labels of the all-potent Express Company. Then the whip cracked, the coach rolled away, and the last traces of the adventurous young couple disappeared in the hanging red dust of its wheels.

But Yuba Bill's grim satisfaction at the happy issue of the episode seemed to suffer no abatement. He even exceeded his usual deliberately regulated potations, and, standing comfortably with his back to the centre of the now deserted barroom, was more than usually loquacious with the Expressman. "You see," he said, in bland reminiscence, "when your old Uncle Bill takes hold of a job like this, he puts it straight through without changin' hosses. Yet thar was a moment, young feller, when I thought I was stompt! It was when we 'd made up our mind to make that chap tell the gal fust all what he was! Ef she 'd rared or kicked in the traces, or hung back only ez much ez that, we 'd hev given him jest five minits' law to get up and get and leave her, and we 'd hev toted that gal and her fixin's back to her dad again! But she jest gave a little scream and start, and then went off inter hysterics, right on his buzzum, laughing and cryin' and sayin' that nothin' should part 'em. Gosh! if I did n't think *he* woz more cut up than she about it; a minit it looked as ef *he* did n't allow to marry her arter all, but that passed, and they was married hard and fast — you bet! I reckon he 's had enough of stayin' out o' nights to last him, and ef the valley settlements hev n't got hold of a very shining member, at least the foothills hev got shut of one more of the Ramon Martinez gang."

"What 's that about the Ramon Martinez gang?" said a quiet potential voice.

Bill turned quickly. It was the voice of the Divisional Superintendent of the Express Company, — a man of eccentric determination of character, and one of the few whom the autocratic Bill recognized as an equal, — who had just entered the barroom. His dusty pongee cloak and soft hat indicated that he had that morning arrived on a round of inspection.

"Don't care if I do, Bill," he continued, in response to Bill's invitatory gesture, walking to the bar. "It's a little raw out on the road. Well, what were you saying about Ramon Martinez gang? You have n't come across one of 'em, have you?"

"No," said Bill, with a slight blinking of his eye, as he ostentatiously lifted his glass to the light.

"And you *won't*," added the Superintendent, leisurely sipping his liquor. "For the fact is, the gang is about played out. Not from want of a job now and then, but from the difficulty of disposing of the results of their work. Since the new instructions to the agents to identify and trace all dust and bullion offered to them went into force, you see, they can't get rid of their swag. All the gang are spotted at the offices, and it costs too much for them to pay a fence or a middleman of any standing. Why, all that flaky river gold they took from the Excelsior Company can be identified as easy as if it was stamped with the company's mark. They can't melt it down themselves; they can't get others to do it for them; they can't ship it to the Mint or Assay Offices in Marysville and 'Frisco, for they won't take it without our certificate and seals; and *we* don't take any undeclared freight *within* the lines that we 've drawn around their beat, except from people and agents known. Why, *you* know that well enough, Jim," he said, suddenly appealing to the Expressman, "don't you?"

Possibly the suddenness of the appeal caused the Expressman to swallow his liquor the wrong way, for he was overtaken with a fit of coughing, and stammered hastily as he laid down his glass, "Yes — of course — certainly."

"No, sir," resumed the Superintendent cheerfully, "they 're pretty well played out. And the best proof of it is that they 've lately been robbing ordinary passengers' trunks. There was a freight wagon 'held up' near Dow's Flat the other day, and a lot of baggage gone through. I had to go down there to look into it. Darned if they had n't lifted a lot o' woman's wedding things from that rich couple who got married the other day out at Marysville. Looks as if they were playing it rather low down, don't it? Coming down to hardpan and the bed rock — eh?"

The Expressman's face was turned anxiously towards Bill, who, after a hurried gulp of his remaining liquor, still stood staring at the window. Then he slowly drew on one of his large gloves. "Ye did n't," he said, with a slow, drawling, but perfectly distinct, articulation, "happen to know old 'Skinner' Hemmings when you were over there?"

"Yes."

"And his daughter?"

"He has n't got any."

"A sort o' mild, innocent, guileless child of nature?" persisted Bill, with a yellow face, a deadly calm and Satanic deliberation.

"No. I tell you he *has n't* any daughter. Old man Hemmings is a confirmed old bachelor. He 's too mean to support more than one."

"And you did n't happen to know any o' that gang, did ye?" continued Bill, with infinite protraction.

"Yes. Knew 'em all. There was French Pete, Cherokee Bob, Kanaka Joe, One-eyed Stillson, Softy Brown, Spanish Jack, and two or three Greasers."

"And ye did n't know a man by the name of Charley Byng?"

"No," returned the Superintendent, with a slight suggestion of weariness and a distraught glance towards the door.

"A dark, stylish chap, with shifty black eyes and a curled-up merstache?" continued Bill, with dry, colorless persistence.

"No. Look here, Bill, I 'm in a little bit of a hurry — but I suppose you must have your little joke before we part. Now, what *is* your little game?"

"Wot you mean?" demanded Bill, with sudden brusqueness.

"Mean? Well, old man, you know as well as I do. You 're giving me the very description of Ramon Martinez himself, ha! ha! No — Bill! you did n't play me this time. You 're mighty spry and clever, but you did n't catch on just then."

He nodded and moved away with a light

laugh.   Bill turned a stony face to the
Expressman.   Suddenly a gleam of mirth
came into his gloomy eyes.   He bent over
the young man, and said in a hoarse, chuckling whisper: —

"But I got even after all!"

"How?"

"He's tied up to that lying little she-
devil, hard and fast!"

THE REFORMATION OF JAMES REDDY.

I.

IT was a freshly furrowed field, so large that the eye at first scarcely took in its magnitude. The irregular surface of up-turned, oily, wave-shaped clods took the appearance of a vast, black, chopping sea, that reached from the actual shore of San Francisco Bay to the low hills of the Coast Range. The sea-breeze that blew chilly over this bleak expanse added to that fancy, and the line of straggling whitewashed farm buildings, that half way across lifted them-selves above it, seemed to be placed on an island in its midst. Even the one or two huge, misshapen agricultural machines, abandoned in the furrows, bore an odd re-semblance to hulks or barges adrift upon its waste.

This marine suggestion was equally no-ticeable from the door of one of the farm buildings — a long, detached wooden shed

— into which a number of farm laborers were slowly filing, although one man was apparently enough impressed by it to linger and gaze over that rigid sea. Except in their rough dress and the labor-stains of soil on their hands and faces, they represented no particular type or class. They were young and old, robust and delicate, dull and intelligent; kept together only by some philosophical, careless, or humorous acceptance of equally enforced circumstance in their labors, as convicts might have been. For they had been picked up on the streets and wharves of San Francisco, — discharged sailors, broken-down miners, helpless new-comers, unemployed professional men, and ruined traders, — to assist in ploughing and planting certain broad leagues of rich alluvial soil for a speculative Joint Stock Company, at a weekly wage that would have made an European peasant independent for half a year. Yet there was no enthusiasm in their labor, although it was seldom marked by absolute laziness or evasion, and was more often hindered by ill-regulated "spurts" and excessive effort, as if the laborer was anxious to get through with it; for in the few confidences they exchanged there was little allusion to the present, and they talked chiefly of what they were going to do when their work was over. They were gregarious only at their meals in one of the sheds, or when at night they sought their "bunks" or berths together in the larger building.

The man who had lingered to look at the dreary prospect had a somewhat gloomy, discontented face, whose sensitive lines indicated a certain susceptibility to such impressions. He was further distinguished by having also lingered longer with the washing of his hands and face in the battered tin basin on a stool beside the door, and by the circumstance that the operation revealed the fact that they were whiter than those of his companions. Drying his fingers slowly on the long roller-towel, he stood gazing with a kind of hard abstraction across the darkening field, the strip of faded colorless shore, and the chill gray sea, to the dividing point of land on the opposite coast, which in the dying daylight was silhouetted against the cold horizon.

He knew that around that point and behind it lay the fierce, half-grown, half-tamed city of yesterday that had worked his ruin.

It was scarcely a year ago that he had plunged into its wildest excesses, — a reckless gambler among speculators, a hopeless speculator among gamblers, — until the little fortune he had brought thither had been swept away.

From time to time he had kept up his failing spirit with the feverish exaltation of dissipation, until, awakening from a drunkard's dream one morning, he had found himself on board a steamboat crossing the bay, in company with a gang of farm laborers with whom he was hired. A bitter smile crossed his lips as his eyes hovered over the cold, rugged fields before him. Yet he knew that they had saved him. The unaccustomed manual labor in the open air, the regular hours, the silent, heavy, passionless nights, the plain but wholesome food, were all slowly restoring his youth and strength again. Temptation and passion had alike fled these unlovely fields and grim employment. Yet he was not grateful. He nursed his dreary convalescence as he had his previous dissipation, as part of a wrong done him by one for whose sake, he was wont to believe, he had sacrificed himself. That person was a woman.

Turning at last from the prospect and his bitter memories to join his companions, he found that they had all passed in. The benches before the long table on which supper was spread were already filled, and he stood in hesitation, looking down the line of silent and hungrily preoccupied men on either side. A young girl, who was standing near a smaller serving-table, apparently assisting an older woman in directing the operation of half a dozen Chinese waiters, moved forward and cleared a place for him at a side-table, pushing before it the only chair in the room, — the one she had lately vacated. As she placed some of the dishes before him with a timid ostentation, and her large but well-shaped hands came suddenly in contact with, and in direst contrast to his own whiter and more delicate ones, she blushed faintly. He lifted his eyes to hers.

He had seen her half a dozen times before, for she was the daughter of the ranch superintendent, and occasionally assisted her mother in this culinary supervision — which did not, however, bring her into any familiar association with the men. Even the younger ones, perhaps from over-consciousness of their inferior position or the preoccupation of their labor, never indulged in any gallantry toward her, and he himself, in his revulsion of feeling against the whole sex, had scarcely noticed that she was good-looking. But this naïve exhibition of preference could not be overlooked, either by his companions, who smiled cynically across the table, or by himself, from whose morbid fancy it struck an ignoble suggestion. Ah, well! the girl was pretty — the daughter of his employer, who rumor said owned a controlling share in the company; why should he not make this chance preference lead to something, if only to ameliorate, in ways like this, his despicable position here. He knew the value of his own good looks, his superior education, and a certain recklessness which women liked; why should he not profit by them as well as the one woman who had brought him to this? He owed her sex nothing; if those among them who were not bad were only fools, there was no reason why he should not deceive them as they had him. There was all this small audacity and cynical purpose in his brown eyes as he deliberately fixed them on hers. And I grieve to say that these abominable sentiments seemed only to impart to them a certain attractive brilliancy, and a determination which the undetermining sex is apt to admire.

She blushed again, dropped her eyes, replied to his significant thanks with a few indistinct words, and drew away from the table with a sudden timidity that was half confession.

She did not approach him again during the meal, but seemed to have taken a sudden interest in the efficiency of the waiters, generally, which she had not shown before. I do not know whether this was merely an effort at concealment, or an awakened recognition of her duty; but, after the fashion of her sex, — and perhaps in contrast to his, — she was kinder that evening to the average man on account of *him.* He did not, however, notice it; nor did her absence interfere with his now healthy appetite; he finished his meal, and only when he rose to take his hat from the peg above him did he glance around the room. Their eyes met again. As he passed out, although it was dark, he put on his hat a little more smartly.

The air was clear and cold, but the outlines of the landscape had vanished. His companions, with the instinct of tired animals, were already making their way in knots of two or three, or in silent file, across the intervening space between the building and their dormitory. A few had already lit their pipes and were walking leisurely, but the majority were hurrying from the chill sea-breeze to the warmth and comfort of the long, well-lit room, lined with blanketed berths, and set with plain wooden chairs and tables. The young man lingered for a moment on the wooden platform outside the dining-shed, — partly to evade this only social gathering of his fellows as they retired for the night, and partly attracted by a strange fascination to the faint distant glow, beyond the point of land, which indicated the lights of San Francisco.

There was a slight rustle behind him! It was the young girl who, with a white woolen scarf thrown over her head and shoulders, had just left the room. She started when she saw him, and for an instant hesitated.

"You are going home, Miss Woodridge?" he said pleasantly.

"Yes," she returned, in a faint, embarrassed voice. "I thought I'd run on ahead of ma!"

"Will you allow me to accompany you?"

"It's only a step," she protested, indicating the light in the window of the superintendent's house, — the most remote of the group of buildings, yet scarcely a quarter of a mile distant.

"But it's quite dark," he persisted smilingly.

She stepped from the platform to the ground; he instantly followed and ranged himself at a little distance from her side. She protested still feebly against his "troubling himself," but in another moment they were walking on quietly together. Nevertheless, a few paces from the platform they came upon the upheaved clods of the fresh furrows, and their progress over them was slow and difficult.

"Shall I help you? Will you take my arm?" he said politely.

"No, thank you, Mr. Reddy."

So! she knew his name! He tried to look into her eyes, but the woolen scarf hid her head. After all, there was nothing strange in her knowing him; she probably

had the names of the men before her in the
dining-room, or on the books. After a
pause he said: —

"You quite startled me. One becomes
such a mere working machine here that
one quite forgets one's own name, — especially with the prefix of 'Mr.'"

"And if it don't happen to be one's real
name either," said the girl, with an odd,
timid audacity.

He looked up quickly — more attracted by
her manner than her words; more amused
than angry.

"But Reddy happens to be my real
name."

"Oh!"

"What made you think it was not?"
The clods over which they were clambering were so uneven that sometimes the
young girl was mounting one at the same
moment that Reddy was descending from
another. Her reply, half muffled in her
shawl, was delivered over his head. "Oh,
because pa says most of the men here don't
give their real names — they don't care to
be known afterward. Ashamed of their
work, I reckon."

His face flushed a moment, even in the

darkness. He *was* ashamed of his work, and perhaps a little of the pitiful sport he was beginning. But oddly enough, the aggressive criticism only whetted his purpose. The girl was evidently quite able to take care of herself; why should he be over-chivalrous?

"It is n't very pleasant to be doing the work of a horse, an ox, or a machine, if you can do other things," he said half seriously.

"But you never used to do anything at all, did you?" she asked.

He hesitated. Here was a chance to give her an affecting history of his former exalted fortune and position, and perhaps even to stir her evidently romantic nature with some suggestion of his sacrifices to one of her own sex. Women liked that sort of thing. It aroused at once their emulation and their condemnation of each other. He seized the opportunity, but — for some reason, he knew not why — awkwardly and clumsily, with a simulated pathos that was lachrymose, a self-assertion that was boastful, and a dramatic manner that was unreal. Suddenly the girl stopped him.

"Yes, I know all *that;* pa told me. Told

me you 'd been given away by some woman."

His face again flushed — this time with
anger. The utter failure of his story to excite her interest, and her perfect possession
of herself and the situation, — so unlike her
conduct a few moments before, — made him
savagely silent, and he clambered on sul-
lenly at her side. Presently she stopped,
balancing herself with a dexterity he could
not imitate on one of the larger upheaved
clods, and said: —

"I was thinking that, as you can't do
much with those hands of yours, digging
and shoveling, and not much with your feet
either, over ploughed ground, you might do
some inside work, that would pay you better, too. You might help in the dining-
room, setting table and washing up, helping ma and me — though *I* don't do much
except overseeing. I could show you what
to do at first, and you 'd learn quick
enough. If you say 'yes,' I 'll speak to pa
to-night. He 'll do whatever I say."

The rage and shame that filled his breast
choked even the bitter laugh that first rose
to his lips. If he could have turned on
his heel and left her with marked indig-

nation, he would have done so, but they were scarcely half way across the field; his stumbling retreat would have only appeared ridiculous, and he was by no means sure that she would not have looked upon it as merely a confession of his inability to keep up with her. And yet there was something peculiarly fascinating and tantalizing in the situation. She did not see the sardonic glitter in his eye as he said brutally : —

"Ha! and that would give me the exquisite pleasure of being near you."

She seemed a little confused, even under her enwrappings, and in stepping down her foot slipped. Reddy instantly scrambled up to her and caught her as she was pitching forward into the furrow. Yet in the struggle to keep his own foothold he was aware that she was assisting him, and although he had passed his arm around her waist, as if for her better security, it was only through *her* firm grasp of his wrists that he regained his own footing. The "cloud" had fallen back from her head and shoulders, her heavy hair had brushed his cheek and left its faint odor in his nostrils; the rounded outline of her figure had been slightly drawn against his own. His mean resentment wavered; her proposition, which at first seemed only insulting, now took a vague form of satisfaction; his ironical suggestion seemed a natural expression. "Well, I say 'yes' then," he said, with an affected laugh. "That is, if you think I can manage to do the work; it is not exactly in my line, you know." Yet he somehow felt that his laugh was feeble and unconvincing.

"Oh, it's easy enough," said the girl quietly. "You've only got to be clean — and that's in your line, I should say."

"And if I thought it would please you," he added, with another attempt at gallantry.

She did not reply, but moved steadily on, he fancied a little more rapidly. They were nearing the house; he felt he was losing time and opportunity. The uneven nature of the ground kept him from walking immediately beside her, unless he held her hand or arm. Yet an odd timidity was overtaking him. Surely this was the same girl whose consciousness and susceptibility were so apparent a moment ago; yet her speech had been inconsistent, unsympathetic, and coldly practical. "It's very kind of you," he began again, scrambling up one side of the furrow as she descended on the other, "to — to — take such an interest in — in a stranger, and I wish you knew how" (she had mounted the ridge again, and stood balancing herself as if waiting for him to finish his sentence) "how — how deeply — I — I" — She dropped quickly down again with the same movement of uneasy consciousness, and he left the sentence unfinished. The house was now only a few yards away ; he hurried forward, but she reached the wooden platform and stoop upon it first. He, however, at the same moment caught her hand.

"I want to thank you," he said, "and say good-night."

"Good-night." Her voice was indistinct again, and she was trembling. Emboldened and reckless, he sprang upon the platform, and encircling her with one arm, with his other hand he unloosed the woolen cloud around her head and bared her faintly flushed cheek and half-open, hurriedly breathing lips. But the next moment she threw her head back with a single powerful movement, and, as it seemed to him, with scarcely an effort cast him off with both hands, and sent him toppling from the platform to the ground. He scrambled quickly to his feet again, flushed, angry, and — frightened! Perhaps she would call her father; he would be insulted, or worse, — laughed at! He had lost even this pitiful chance of bettering his condition. But he was as relieved as he was surprised to see that she was standing quietly on the edge of the platform, apparently waiting for him to rise. Her face was still uncovered, still slightly flushed, but bearing no trace of either insult or anger. When he stood erect again, she looked at him gravely and drew the woolen cloud over her head, as she said calmly, "Then I 'll tell pa you 'll take the place, and I reckon you 'll begin to-morrow morning."

II.

Angered, discomfited, and physically and morally beaten, James . Reddy stumbled and clambered back across the field. The beam of light that had streamed out over the dark field as the door opened and shut on the girl left him doubly confused and bewildered. In his dull anger and mortification, there seemed only one course for him to pursue. He would demand his wages in the morning, and cut the whole concern. He would go back to San Francisco and work there, where he at least had friends who respected his station. Yet, he ought to have refused the girl's offer before she had repulsed him; his retreat now meant nothing, and might even tempt her, in her vulgar pique, to reveal her rebuff of him. He raised his eyes mechanically, and looked gloomily across the dark waste and distant bay to the opposite shore. But the fog had already hidden the glow of the city's lights, and, thickening around the horizon, seemed to be slowly hemming him in with the dreary rancho. In his present frame of mind there was a certain fatefulness in this that precluded his once free agency, and to that extent relieved and absolved *him* of any choice. He reached the dormitory and its turned-down lights in a state of tired and dull uncertainty, for which sleep seemed to offer the only relief. He rolled himself in his blankets with an animal instinct of comfort and shut his eyes, but their sense appeared to open upon Nelly Woodridge as she stood looking down upon him from the platform. Even through the dull pain of his bruised susceptibilities he was conscious of a strange satisfaction he had not felt before. He fell asleep at last, to waken only to the sunlight streaming through the curtainless windows on his face. To his surprise the long shed was empty and deserted, except for a single Chinaman who was sweeping the floor at the farther end. As Reddy started up, the man turned and approached him with a characteristic, vague, and patient smile.

"All lity, John, you sleepee heap! Mistel Woodlidge he say you no go wolkee field allee same Mellikan man. You stoppee inside housee allee same *me*. Shabbee? You come to glubbee [grub] now" (pointing to the distant dining-shed), "and then you washee dish."

The full extent of his new degradation flashed upon Reddy with this added insult of his brother menial's implicit equality. He understood it all. He had been detached from the field-workers and was to come to a later breakfast, perhaps the broken victuals of the first repast, and wash the dishes. He remembered his new bargain. Very well! he would refuse positively, take his dismissal, and leave that morning! He hurriedly dressed himself, and followed the Chinaman into the open air.

The fog still hung upon the distant bay and hid the opposite point. But the sun shone with dry Californian brilliancy over the league - long field around him, revealing every detail of the rancho with sharp, matter of fact directness, and without the least illusion of distance or romance. The rough, unplaned, unpainted walls of the dinner-shed stood out clearly before him; the half-filled buckets of water on the near platform, and the immense tubs piled with dirty dishes. He scowled darkly as he walked forward, conscious, nevertheless, of the invigorating discipline of the morning air and the wholesome whip in the sky above him. He entered sharply and aggressively. To his relief, the room at first sight seemed, like the dormitory he had just left, to be empty. But a voice, clear, dry, direct, and practical as the morning itself, spoke in his ear: "Mornin', Reddy! My daughter says you 're willin' to take an indoor job, and I reckon, speakin' square, as man to man, it 's more in your line than what you 've bin doin'. It may n't be high-toned work, but work 's *work* anyhow you can fix it; and the only difference I kin see is in the work that a man does squarely, and the work that he shirks."

"But," said Reddy hurriedly, "there 's a mistake. I came here only to "—

"Work like the others, I understand. Well, you see you *can't*. You do your best, I know. I ain't findin' fault, but it ain't in your line. *This* is, and the pay is better."

"But," stammered Reddy, "Miss Woodridge did n't understand "—

" Yes, she did," returned Woodridge impatiently, "and she told me. She says she 'll show you round at first. You 'll catch on all right. Sit down and eat your breakfast, and she 'll be along before you 're through. Ez for *me*, I must get up and get. So long!" and before Reddy had an opportunity to continue his protest, he turned away.

The young man glanced vexatiously around him. A breakfast much better in service and quality than the one he had been accustomed to smoked on the table. There was no one else in the room. He could hear the voices of the Chinese waiters in the kitchen beyond. He was healthily hungry, and after a moment's hesitation sat down and began his meal. He could expostulate with her afterward, and withdraw his promise. He was entitled to his breakfast, anyway!

Once or twice, while thus engaged, he heard the door of the kitchen open and the clipping tread of the Chinese waiters, who deposited some rattling burden on the adjacent tables, but he thought it prudent not to seem to notice them. When he had finished, the pleasant, hesitating, boyish contralto of Miss Woodridge fell upon his ear.

"When you 're ready, I 'll show you how to begin your work."

He turned quickly, with a flush of mortification at being discovered at his repast, and his anger returned. But as his eyes fell upon her delicately colored but tranquil face, her well-shaped figure, coquettishly and spotlessly cuffed, collared, and aproned, and her clear blue but half-averted eyes, he again underwent a change. She certainly was very pretty — that most seductive prettiness which seemed to be warmed into life by her consciousness of himself. Why should he take her or himself so seriously? Why not play out the farce, and let those who would criticise him and think his acceptance of the work degrading understand that it was only an affair of gallantry. He could afford to serve Woodridge at least a few weeks for the favor of this Rachel! Forgetful of his rebuff of the night before, he fixed his brown eyes on hers with an audacious levity.

"Oh yes — the work! Let us see it. I 'm ready in name and nature for anything that Miss Woodridge wants of me. I 'm just dying to begin."

His voice was raised slightly, with a high comedy jauntiness, for the benefit of the Chinese waiters who might be lingering to see the "Mellican man" assume their functions. But it failed in effect. With their characteristic calm acceptance of any eccentricity in a "foreign devil," they scarcely lifted their eyes. The young girl pointed to a deep basket filled with dishes which had been placed on the larger table, and said, without looking at Reddy: —

"You had better begin by 'checking' the crockery. That is, counting the pieces separately and then arranging them in sets

as they come back from washing. There's
the book to compare them with and to set
down what is broken, missing, or chipped.
You'll have a clean towel with you to wipe
the pieces that have not been cleaned
enough; or, if they are too dirty, you'll
send them back to the kitchen."

"Couldn't I wash them myself?" said
Reddy, continuing his ostentatious levity.

"Not yet," said the girl, with grave hesitation; "you'd break them."

She stood watching him, as with affected
hilarity he began to take the dishes from
the basket. But she noticed that in spite
of this jocular simulation his grasp was firm
and delicate, and that there was no clatter
— which would have affected her sensitive
ear — as he put them down. She laid a
pencil and account book beside him and
turned away.

"But you are not going?" he said, in
genuine surprise.

"Yes," she said quietly, "until you get
through 'checking.' Then I'll come back
and show you what you have to do next.
You're getting on very well."

"But that was because you were with
me."

She colored slightly and, without looking at him, moved slowly to the door and disappeared.

Reddy went back to his work, disappointed but not discomfited. He was getting accustomed to the girl's eccentricities. Whether it was the freshness of the morning air and sunlight streaming in at the open windows, the unlooked-for solitude and security of the empty room, or that there was nothing really unpleasant in his occupation, he went on cheerfully "checking" the dishes, narrowly examining them for chips and cracks, and noting them in the book. Again discovering that a few were imperfectly cleaned and wiped, he repaired the defect with cold water and a towel without the least thought of the operation being degrading. He had finished his task in half an hour; she had not returned; why should he not go on and set the table? As he straightened and turned the coarse table-cloth, he made the discovery that the long table was really composed of half a dozen smaller ones, and that the hideous parallelogram which had always so offended him was merely the outcome of carelessness and want of taste. Without a moment's hesitation he set at work to break up the monotonous line and rearranged the tables laterally, with small open spaces between them. The task was no light one, even for a stronger man, but he persevered in it with a new-found energy until he had changed the whole aspect of the room. It looked larger, wider, and less crowded; its hard, practical, workhouse-like formality had disappeared. He had paused to survey it, panting still with his unusual exertion, when a voice broke upon his solitude.

"Well, I wanter know!"

The voice was not Nelly's, but that of her mother, — a large-boned, angular woman of fifty, — who had entered the room unperceived. The accents were simply those of surprise, but on James Reddy's present sensitive mood, coupled with the feeling that here was a new witness to his degradation, he might have resented it; but he detected the handsome, reserved figure of the daughter a few steps behind her. Their eyes met; wonderful to relate, the young girl's no longer evaded him, but looked squarely into his with a bright expression of pleasure he had not seen before. He checked himself with a sudden thrill of gratification.

" Well, I declare," continued Mrs. Woodridge; "is that *your* idea — or yours, Helen ? "

Here Reddy simply pointed out the advantages for serving afforded by the new arrangement ; that all the tables were equally and quickly accessible from the serving-table and sideboard, and that it was no longer necessary to go the whole length of the room to serve the upper table. He tactfully did not refer to the improved appearance of the room.

"Well, as long as it ain't mere finikin," said the lady graciously, " and seems to bring the folks and their vittles nearer together — we 'll try it to-day. It does look kinder *cityfied* — and I reckoned that was all the good it was. But I calkilated you were goin' to check the crockery this morning."

"It 's done," said Reddy, smilingly handing her the account-book.

Mrs. Woodridge glanced over it, and then surveyed her new assistant.

"And you did n't find any plates that were dirty and that had to be sent back ? "

"Yes, two or three, but I cleaned them myself."

Mrs. Woodridge glanced at him with a look of approving curiosity, but his eyes were just then seeking her daughter's for a more grateful sympathy. All of which the good lady noted, and as it apparently answered the unasked question in her own mind, she only uttered the single exclamation, "Humph!"

But the approbation he received later at dinner, in the satisfaction of his old companions with the new arrangement, had also the effect of diverting from him the criticism he had feared they would make in finding him installed as an assistant to Mrs. Woodridge. On the contrary, they appeared only to recognize in him some especial and superior faculty utilized for their comfort, and when the superintendent, equally pleased, said it was "all Reddy's own idea," no one doubted that it was this particular stroke of genius which gained him the obvious promotion. If he had still thought of offering his flirtation with Nelly as an excuse, there was now no necessity for any. Having shown to his employers his capacity for the highest and lowest work, they naturally preferred to use his best abilities — and he was kept from any menial service. His accounts were so carefully and intelligently rendered that the entire care .of the building and its appointments was intrusted to him. At the end of the week Mr. Woodridge took him aside.

"I say, you ain't got any job in view arter you finish up here, hev ye?"

Reddy started. Scarcely ten days ago he had a hundred projects, schemes, and speculations, more or less wild and extravagant, wherewith he was to avenge and recoup himself in San Francisco. Now they were gone — he knew not where and how. He briefly said he had not.

"Because," continued Woodridge, "I 've got an idea of startin' a hotel in the Oak Grove, just on the slope back o' the rancho. The company 's bound to make some sort o' settlement there for the regular hands, and the place is pooty enough for 'Frisco people who want to run over here and get set up for a day or two. Thar 's plenty of wood and water up thar, and the company 's sure to have a wharf down on the shore. I 'll provide the capital, if you will put in your time. You can sling in ez much style as you like there" (this was an allusion to Reddy's attempt to enliven the blank walls

with colored pictures from the illustrated
papers and green ceanothus sprays from the
slope); "in fact, the more style the better
for them city folks. Well, you think it
over."

He did. But meantime he seemed to
make little progress in his court of the superintendent's daughter. He tried to think
it was because he had allowed himself to
be diverted by his work, but although she
always betrayed the same odd physical consciousness of his presence, it was certain
that she never encouraged him. She gave
him the few directions that his new occupation still made necessary, and looked her
approval of his success. But nothing more.
He was forced to admit that this was exactly
what she might have done as the superintendent's daughter to a deserving employee.
Whereat, for a few days he assumed an air
of cold and ceremonious politeness, until
perceiving that, far from piquing the girl,
it seemed to gratify her, and even to render
her less sensitive in his company, he sulked
in good earnest. This proving ineffective
also, — except to produce a kind of com-
passionate curiosity, — his former dull rage
returned. The planting of the rancho was

nearly over; his service would be ended next week; he had not yet given his answer to Woodridge's proposition; he would decline it and cut the whole concern!

It was a crisp Sunday morning. The breakfast hour was later on that day to allow the men more time for their holiday, which, however, they generally spent in cards, gossip, or reading in their sleeping-sheds. It usually delayed Reddy's work, but as he cared little for the companionship of his fellows, it enabled him, without a show of unsociability, to seclude himself in the dining-room. And this morning he was early approached by his employer.

"I'm goin' to take the women folks over to Oakdale to church," said Mr. Woodridge; "ef ye keer to join us thar's a seat in the wagon, and I'll turn on a couple of Chinamen to do the work for you, just now; and Nelly or the old woman will give you a lift this afternoon with the counting up."

Reddy felt instinctively that the invitation had been instigated by the young girl. A week before he would have rejoiced at it; a month ago he would have accepted it if only as a relief to his degraded position, but in the pique of this new passion he

almost rudely declined it. An hour later
he saw Nelly, becomingly and even tastefully dressed, — with the American girl's
triumphant superiority to her condition and
surroundings, — ride past in her father's
smart "carryall." He was startled to see
that she looked so like a lady. Then, with
a new and jealous inconsistency, significant
of the progress of his passion, he resolved
to go to church too. She should see that
he was not going to remain behind like a
mere slave. He remembered that he had
still certain remnants of his past finery in
his trunk; he would array himself in them,
walk to Oakdale, and make one of the
congregation. He managed to change his
clothes without attracting the attention of
his fellows, and set out.

The air was pure but keen, with none of
the languor of spring in its breath, although
a few flowers were beginning to star the
weedy wagon-tracked lane, and there was
an awakening spice in the wayside southern-
wood and myrtle. He felt invigorated,
although it seemed only to whet his jealous
pique. He hurried on without even glancing toward the distant coast-line of San
Francisco or even thinking of it. The bit-

ter memories of the past had been obliterated by the bitterness of the present. He no longer thought of "that woman;" even when he had threatened to himself to return to San Francisco, he was vaguely conscious that it was not *she* who was again drawing him there, but Nelly who was driving him away.

The service was nearly over when he arrived at the chilly little corrugated-zinc church at Oakdale, but he slipped into one of the back seats. A few worshipers turned round to look at him. Among them were the daughters of a neighboring miller, who were slightly exercised over the unusual advent of a good-looking stranger with certain exterior signs of elegance. Their excitement was communicated by some mysterious instinct to their neighbor, Nelly Woodridge. She also turned and caught his eye. But to all appearances she not only showed no signs of her usual agitation at his presence, but did not seem to even recognize him. In the acerbity of his pique he was for a moment gratified at what he believed to be the expression of her wounded pride, but his uneasiness quickly returned, and at the conclusion of the service he slipped out of the church with one or two of the more restless in the congregation. As he passed through the aisle he heard the escort of the miller's daughters, in response to a whispered inquiry, say distinctly: "Only the head - waiter over at the company's rancho." Whatever hesitating idea Reddy might have had of waiting at the church door for the appearance of Nelly vanished before the brutal truth. His brow darkened, and with flushed cheeks he turned his back upon the building and plunged into the woods. This time there was no hesitation in his resolve; he would leave the rancho at the expiration of his engagement. Even in a higher occupation he felt he could never live down his reputation there.

In his morose abstraction he did not know how long or how aimlessly he had wandered among the mossy live-oaks, his head and shoulders often imperiled by the down-curving of some huge knotted limb; his feet straying blindly from the faint track over the thickly matted carpet of chickweed which hid their roots. But it was nearly an hour before he emerged upon a wide, open, wooded slope, and, from the distant view of field and shore, knew that he was at Oak Grove, the site of Woodridge's projected hotel. And there, surely, at a little distance, was the Woodridges' wagon and team tied up to a sapling, while the superintendent and his wife were slowly climbing the slope, and apparently examining the prospect. Without waiting to see if Nelly was with them, Reddy instantly turned to avoid meeting them. But he had not proceeded a hundred yards before he came upon that young lady, who had evidently strayed from the party, and who was now unconsciously advancing toward him. A *rencontre* was inevitable.

She started slightly, and then stopped, with all her old agitation and embarrassment. But, to his own surprise, he was also embarrassed and even tongue-tied.

She spoke first.

"You were at church. I did n't quite know you in — in — these clothes."

In her own finery she had undergone such a change to Reddy's consciousness that he, for the first time in their acquaintance, now addressed her as on his own level, and as if she had no understanding of his own feelings.

"Oh," he said, with easy bitterness, "*others* did, if you did not. They all detected the 'head-waiter' at the Union Company's rancho. Even if I had accepted your kindness in offering me a seat in your wagon it would have made no difference." He was glad to put this construction on his previous refusal, for in the new relations which seemed to be established by their Sunday clothes he was obliged to soften the churlishness of that refusal also.

"I don't think you'd look nice setting the table in kid gloves," she said, glancing quickly at his finery as if accepting it as the real issue; "but you can wear what you like at other times. *I* never found fault with your working clothes."

There was such a pleasant suggestion in her emphasis that his ill-humor softened. Her eyes wandered over the opposite grove, where her unconscious parents had just disappeared.

"Papa's very keen about the hotel," she continued, "and is going to have the workmen break ground to-morrow. He says he'll have it up in two months and ready to open, if he has to make the men work double time. When you're manager, you won't mind what folks say."

There was no excuse for his further hesitation. He must speak out, but he did it in a half-hearted way.

"But if I simply go away — *without* being manager — I won't hear their criticism either."

"What do you mean?" she said quickly.

"I 've — I 've been thinking of — of going back to San Francisco," he stammered awkwardly.

A slight flush of contemptuous indignation passed over her face, and gave it a strength and expression he had never seen there before. "Oh, you 've not reformed yet, then?" she said, under her scornful lashes.

"I don't understand you," he said, flushing.

"Father ought to have told you," she went on dryly, "that that woman has gone off to the Springs with her husband, and you won't see *her* at San Francisco."

"I don't know what you mean — and your father seems to take an unwarrantable interest in my affairs," said Reddy, with an anger that he was conscious, however, was half simulated.

"No more than he ought to, if he expects

to trust you with all *his* affairs," said the girl shortly; "but you had better tell him you have changed your mind at once, before he makes any further calculations on your staying. He 's just over the hill there, with mother."

She turned away coldly as she spoke, but moved slowly and in the direction of the hill, although she took a less direct trail than the one she had pointed to him. But he followed her, albeit still embarrassedly, and with that new sense of respect which had checked his former surliness. There was her strong, healthy, well-developed figure moving before him, but the modish gray dress seemed to give its pronounced outlines something of the dignity of a goddess. Even the firm hands had the distinguishment of character.

" You understand," he said apologetically, "that I mean no discourtesy to your father or his offer. And " — he hesitated — "neither is my reason what you would infer."

"Then what is it?" she asked, turning to him abruptly. "You know you have no other place when you leave here, nor any chance as good as the one father offers you.

You are not fit for any other work, and you know it. You have no money to speculate with, nor can you get any. If you could, you would have never stayed here."

He could not evade the appalling truthfulness of her clear eyes. He knew it was no use to lie to her; she had evidently thoroughly informed herself regarding his past; more than that, she seemed to read his present thoughts. But not all of them! No! he could startle her still! It was desperate, but he had nothing now to lose. And she liked the truth, — she should have it!

"You are right," he said shortly; "these are not my reasons."

"Then what reason have you?"

"You!"

"Me?" she repeated incredulously, yet with a rising color.

"Yes, *you!* I cannot stay here, and have you look down upon me."

"I don't look down on you," she said simply, yet without the haste of repelling an unjust accusation. "Why should I? Mother and I have done the same work that you are doing, — if that's what you mean ; and father, who is a man like yourself, helped us at first, until he could do other things better." She paused. "Perhaps you think so because *you* looked down on us when you first came here."

"But I did n't," said Reddy quickly.

"You did," said the young girl quietly. "That's why you acted toward me as you did the night you walked home with me. You would not have behaved in that way to any San Francisco young lady — and I'm not one of your — fast — *married women.*"

Reddy felt the hot blood mount to his cheek, and looked away. "I was foolish and rude — and I think you punished me at the time," he stammered. "But you see I was right in saying you looked down on me," he concluded triumphantly.

This was at best a feeble *sequitur*, but the argument of the affections is not always logical. And it had its effect on the girl.

"I was n't thinking of *that*," she said. "It's that you don't know your own mind."

"If I said that I would stay and accept your father's offer, would you think that I did?" he asked quickly.

"I should wait and see what you actually *did* do," she replied.

"But if I stayed — and — and — if I told you that I stayed on *your* account — to be with you and near you only — would you think that a proof?" He spoke hesitatingly, for his lips were dry with a nervousness he had not known before.

"I might, if you told father you expected to be engaged on those terms. For it concerns *him* as much as me. And *he* engages you, and not I. Otherwise I'd think it was only your talk."

Reddy looked at her in astonishment. There was not the slightest trace of coyness, coquetry, or even raillery in her clear, honest eyes, and yet it would seem as if she had taken his proposition in its fullest sense as a matrimonial declaration, and actually referred him to her father. He was pleased, frightened, and utterly unprepared.

"But what would *you* say, Nelly?" He drew closer to her and held out both his hands. But she retreated a step and slipped her own behind her.

"Better see what father says first," she said quietly. "You may change your mind again and go back to San Francisco."

He was confused, and reddened again. But he had become accustomed to her ways; rather, perhaps, he had begun to recognize the quaint justice that underlaid them, or, possibly, some better self of his own, that had been buried under bitterness and sloth and struggled into life. " But whatever he says," he returned eagerly, "cannot alter my feelings to *you*. It can only alter my position here, and you say you are above being influenced by that. Tell me, Nelly —dear Nelly! have you nothing to say to me, *as I am*, or is it only to your father's manager that you would speak?" His voice had an unmistakable ring of sincerity in it, and even startled him — half rascal as he was!

The young girl's clear, scrutinizing eyes softened; her red resolute lips trembled slightly and then parted, the upper one hovering a little to one side over her white teeth. It was Nelly's own peculiar smile, and its serious piquancy always thrilled him. But she drew a little farther back from his brightening eyes, her hands still curled behind her, and said, with the faintest coquettish toss of her head toward the hill: "If you want to see father, you 'd better hurry up."

With a sudden determination as new to him as it was incomprehensible, Reddy turned from her and struck forward in the direction of the hill. He was not quite sure what he was going for. Yet that he, who had only a moment before fully determined to leave the rancho and her, was now going to her father to demand her hand as a contingency of his remaining did not strike him as so extravagant and unexpected a *denouement* as it was a difficult one. He was only concerned *how*, and in what way, he should approach him. In a moment of embarrassment he hesitated, turned, and looked behind him.

She was standing where he had left her, gazing after him, leaning forward with her hands still held behind her. Suddenly, as with an inspiration, she raised them both, carried them impetuously to her lips, blew him a dozen riotous kisses, and then, lowering her head like a colt, whisked her skirt behind her, and vanished in the cover.

III.

It was only May, but the freshness of early summer already clothed the great fields of the rancho. The old resemblance to a sea was still there, more accented, perhaps, by the undulations of bluish-green grain that rolled from the actual shore-line to the foothills. The farm buildings were half submerged in this glowing tide of color and lost their uncouth angularity with their hidden rude foundations. The same sea-breeze blew chilly and steadily from the bay, yet softened and subdued by the fresh odors of leaf and flower. The outlying fringe of oaks were starred through their underbrush with anemones and dog-roses; there were lupines growing rankly in the open spaces, and along the gentle slopes of Oak Grove daisies were already scattered. And, as if it were part of this vernal efflorescence, the eminence itself was crowned with that latest flower of progress and improvement, — the new Oak Grove Hotel!

Long, low, dazzling with white colonnades, verandas, and balconies which retained, however, enough of the dampness of recent creation to make them too cool for loungers, except at high noon, the hotel nevertheless had the charms of freshness, youth, and cleanliness. Reddy's fastidious neatness showed itself in all the appointments, from the mirrored and marbled bar-room, gilded parlors, and snowy dining-room, to the chintz and maple furnishing of the bedrooms above. Reddy's taste, too, had selected the pretty site; his good fortune had afterward discovered in an adjoining thicket a spring of blandly therapeutic qualities. A complaisant medical faculty of San Francisco attested to its merits; a sympathetic press advertised the excellence of the hotel; a novelty-seeking, fashionable circle — as yet without laws and blindly imitative — found the new hotel an admirable variation to the vulgar ordinary "across the bay" excursion, and an accepted excuse for a novel social dissipation. A number of distinguished people had already visited it; certain exclusive families had secured the best rooms; there were a score of pretty women to be seen in its parlors; there had already been a slight scandal. Nothing seemed wanting to insure its success.

Reddy was passing through the little wood where four months before he had parted from Nelly Woodridge to learn his fate from her father. He remembered that interview to which Nelly's wafted kiss had inspired him. He recalled to-day, as he had many times before, the singular complacency with which Mr. Woodridge had received his suit, as if it were a slight and unimportant detail of the business in hand, and how he had told him that Nelly and her mother were going to the "States" for a three months' visit, but that after her return, if they were both "still agreed," he, Woodridge, would make no objection. He remembered the slight shock which this announcement of Nelly's separation from him during his probationary labors had given him, and his sudden suspicion that he had been partly tricked of his preliminary intent to secure her company to solace him. But he had later satisfied himself that she knew nothing of her father's intentions at the time, and he was fain to content himself with a walk through the fields at her side the day she departed, and a single kiss — which left him cold. And now in a few days she would return to witness the successful fufillment of his labors, and — reward him!

It was certainly a complacent prospect. He could look forward to a sensible, prosperous, respectable future. He had won back his good name, his fortune, and position, — not perhaps exactly in the way he had expected, — and he had stilled the wanton, foolish cravings of his passionate nature in the calm, virginal love of an honest, handsome girl who would make him a practical helpmeet, and a comfortable, trustworthy wife. He ought to be very happy. He had never known such perfect health before; he had lost his reckless habits; his handsome, nervous face had grown more placid and contented; his long curls had been conventionally clipped; he had gained flesh unmistakably, and the lower buttons of the slim waistcoat he had worn to church that memorable Sunday were too tight for comfort or looks. *He was* happy; yet as he glanced over the material spring landscape, full of practical health, blossom, and promise of fruition, it struck him that the breeze that blew over it was chilly, even if healthful; and he shivered slightly.

He reached the hotel, entered the office, glanced at the register, and passed through into his private room. He had been away for two days, and noticed with gratification that the influx of visitors was still increasing. His clerk followed into the room.

"There's a lady in 56 who wanted to see you when you returned. She asked particularly for the manager."

"Who is she?"

"Don't know. It's a Mrs. Merrydew, from Sacramento. Expecting her husband on the next steamer."

"Humph! You'll have to be rather careful about these solitary married women. We don't want another scandal, you know."

"She asked for you by name, sir, and I thought you might know her," returned the clerk.

"Very well. I'll go up."

He sent a waiter ahead to announce him, and leisurely mounted the stairs. No. 56 was the sitting-room of a private suite on the first floor. The waiter was holding the door open. As he approached it a faint perfume from the interior made him turn pale. But he recovered his presence of mind sufficiently to close the door sharply upon the waiter behind him.

"Jim," said a voice which thrilled him.

He looked up and beheld what any astute reader of romance will have already suspected — the woman to whom he believed he owed his ruin in San Francisco. She was as beautiful and alluring as ever, albeit she was thinner and more spiritual than he had ever seen her. She was tastefully dressed, as she had always been, a certain style of languorous silken *deshabille* which she was wont to affect in better health now became her paler cheek and feverishly brilliant eyes. There was the same opulence of lace and ornament, and, whether by accident or design, clasped around the slight wrist of her extended hand was a bracelet which he remembered had swept away the last dregs of his fortune.

He took her hand mechanically, yet knowing whatever rage was in his heart he had not the strength to refuse it.

"They told me it was Mrs. Merrydew," he stammered.

"That was my mother's name," she said, with a little laugh. "I thought you knew it. But perhaps you did n't. When I got my divorce from Dick — you did n't know that either, I suppose; it 's three months ago, — I did n't care to take my maiden name again; too many people remembered it. So after the decree was made I called myself Mrs. Merrydew. You had disappeared. They said you had gone East."

"But the clerk says you are expecting your *husband* on the steamer. What does this mean? Why did you tell him that?" He had so far collected himself that there was a ring of inquisition in his voice.

"Oh, I had to give him some kind of reason for my being alone when I did not find you as I expected," she said half wearily. Then a change came over her tired face; a smile of mingled audacity and tentative coquetry lit up the small features. "Perhaps it is true; perhaps I may have a husband coming on the steamer — that depends. Sit down, Jim."

She let his hand drop, and pointed to an armchair from which she had just risen, and sank down herself in a corner of the sofa, her thin fingers playing with and drawing themselves through the tassels of the cushion.

"You see, Jim, as soon as I was free, Louis Sylvester — you remember Louis Sylvester? — wanted to marry me, and even thought that he was the cause of· Dick's divorcing me. He actually went East to settle up some property he had left him there, and he 's coming on the steamer."

"Louis Sylvester!" repeated Reddy, staring at her. "Why, he was a bigger fool than I was, and a worse man!" he added bitterly.

"I believe he was," said the lady, smiling, "and I think he still is. But," she added, glancing at Reddy under her light fringed lids, "you — you 're regularly reformed, are n't you? You 're stouter, too, and altogether more solid and commercial looking. Yet who 'd have thought of your keeping a hotel or ever doing anything but speculate in wild-cat or play at draw poker. How did you drift into it? Come, tell me! I 'm not Mrs. Sylvester just yet, and maybe I might like to go into the business too. You don't want a partner, do you?"

Her manner was light and irresponsible, or rather it suggested a childlike putting of all responsibility for her actions upon others, which he remembered now too well. Perhaps it was this which kept him from observing that the corners of her smiling lips, however, twitched slightly, and that her fingers, twisting the threads of the tassel, were occasionally stiffened nervously. For he burst out: Oh yes; he had drifted into it when it was a toss up if it was n't his body instead that would be found drifting out to sea from the first wharf of San Francisco. Yes, he had been a common laborer, — a farm hand, in those fields she had passed, — a waiter in the farm kitchen, and but for luck he might be taking her orders now in this very hotel. It was not her fault if he was not in the gutter.

She raised her thin hand with a tired gesture as if to ward off the onset of his words. "The same old Jim," she repeated; "and yet I thought you had forgotten all that now, and become calmer and more sensible since you had taken flesh and grown so matter of fact. You ought to have known then, as you know now, that I never could have been anything to you as long as I was tied to Dick. And you know you forced your presents on me, Jim. I took them from *you* because I would take nothing from Dick, for I hated him. And I never knew positively that you were in straits then; you know you always talked big, Jim, and were always going to make your fortune with the next thing you had in hand!"

It was true, and he remembered it. He had not intended this kind of recrimination, but he was exasperated with her wearied acceptance of his reproaches and by a sudden conviction that his long-cherished grievance against her now that he had voiced it was inadequate, mean, and trifling. Yet he could not help saying: —

"Then you had presents from Sylvester, too. I presume you did not hate him, either?"

"He would have married me the day after I got my divorce."

"And so would I," burst out Reddy.

She looked at him fixedly. "You would?" she said with a peculiar emphasis. "And now"—

He colored. It had been part of his revengeful purpose on seeing her to tell her of his engagement to Nelly. He now found himself tongue-tied, irresolute, and ashamed. Yet he felt she was reading his innermost thoughts.

She, however, only lowered her eyes, and with the same tired expression said: "No matter now. Let us talk of something nearer. That was two months ago. And so you have charge of this hotel! I like it so much. I mean the place itself. I fancy I could live here forever. It is so far away and restful. I am so sick of towns and cities, and people. And this little grove is so secluded. If one had merely a little cottage here, one might be so happy."

What did she mean?—what did she expect?—what did she think of doing? She must be got rid of before Nelly's arrival, and yet he found himself wavering under her potent and yet scarcely exerted influence. The desperation of weakness is apt to be more brutal than the determination of strength. He remembered why he had come upstairs, and blurted out: "But you can't stay here. The rules are very stringent in regard to — to strangers like yourself. It will be known who you really are and what people say of you. Even your divorce will tell against you. It's all wrong, I know — but what can I do? I didn't make the rules. I am only a servant of the landlord, and must carry them out."

She leaned back against the sofa and laughed silently. But she presently recovered herself, although with the same expression of fatigue. "Don't be alarmed, my poor Jim! If you mean your friend, Mr. Woodridge, I know him. It was he, himself, who suggested my coming here. And don't misunderstand him — nor me either. He's only a good friend of Sylvester's; they had some speculation together. He's coming here to see me after Louis arrives. He's waiting in San Francisco for his wife and daughter, who come on the same steamer. So you see you won't get into trouble on my account. Don't look so scared, my dear boy."

"Does he know that you knew me?" said Reddy, with a white face.

"Perhaps. But then that was three months ago," returned the lady, smiling, "and you know how you have reformed since, and grown ever so much more steady and respectable."

"Did he talk to you of me?" continued Reddy, still aghast.

"A little — complimentary of course. Don't look so frightened. I didn't give you away."

Her laugh suddenly ceased, and her face changed into a more nervous activity as she rose and went toward the window. She had heard the sound of wheels outside — the coach had just arrived.

"There's Mr. Woodridge now," she said in a more animated voice. "The steamer must be in. But I don't see Louis; do you?"

She turned to where Reddy was standing, but he was gone.

The momentary animation of her face

changed. She lifted her shoulders with a half gesture of scorn, but in the midst of it suddenly threw herself on the sofa, and buried her face in her hands.

A few moments elapsed with the bustle of arrival in the hall and passages. Then there was a hesitating step at her door. She quickly passed her handkerchief over her wet eyes and resumed her former look of weary acceptation. The door opened. But it was Mr. Woodridge who entered. The rough shirt-sleeved ranchman had developed, during the last four months, into an equally blunt but soberly dressed proprietor. His keen energetic face, however, wore an expression of embarrassment and anxiety, with an added suggestion of a half humorous appreciation of it.

"I would n't have disturbed you, Mrs. Merrydew," he said, with a gentle bluntness, "if I had n't wanted to ask your advice before I saw Reddy. I 'm keeping out of his way until I could see you. I left Nelly and her mother in 'Frisco. There 's been some queer goings-on on the steamer coming home; Nelly has sprung a new game on her mother, and — and suthin' that looks as if there might be a new deal.

However," here a sense that he was, perhaps, treating his statement too seriously, stopped him, and he smiled reassuringly, "that is as may be."

"I don't know," he went on, "as I ever told you anything about my Nelly and Reddy, — partik'lerly about Nelly. She's a good girl, a square girl, but she's got some all-fired romantic ideas in her head. Mebbee it kem from her reading, mebbee it kem from her not knowing other girls, or seeing too much of a queer sort of men; but she got an interest in the bad ones, and thought it was her mission to reform them, — reform them by pure kindness, attentive little sisterly ways, and moral example. She first tried her hand on Reddy. When he first kem to us he was — well, he was a blazin' ruin! She took him in hand, yanked him outer himself, put his foot on the bedrock, and made him what you see him now. Well — what happened; why, he got reg'larly soft on her; wanted to *marry her*, and I agreed conditionally, of course, to keep him up to the mark. Did you speak?"

"No," said the lady, with her bright eyes fixed upon him.

"Well, that was all well and good, and I'd liked to have carried out my part of the contract, and was willing, and am still. But you see, Nelly, after she'd landed Reddy on firm ground, got a little tired, I reckon, gal-like, of the thing she'd worked so easily, and when she went East she looked around for some other wreck to try her hand on, and she found it on the steamer coming back. And who do you think it was? Why, our friend Louis Sylvester!"

Mrs. Merrydew smiled slightly, with her bright eyes still on the speaker.

"Well, you know he *is* fast at times — if he is a friend of mine — and she reg'larly tackled him; and as my old woman says, it was a sight to see her go for him. But then *he* did n't tumble to it. No! Reformin' ain't in *his* line I 'm afeard. And what was the result? Why, Nelly only got all the more keen when she found she could n't manage him like Reddy, — and, between you and me, she 'd have liked Reddy more if he had n't been so easy, — and it 's ended, I reckon, in her now falling dead in love with Sylvester. She swears she won't marry any one else, and wants to devote her whole life to him! Now, what's to be done! Reddy don't know it yet, and I don't know how to tell him. Nelly says her mission was ended when she made a new man of him, and he oughter be thankful for that. Couldn't you kinder break the news to him and tell him there ain't any show for him?"

"Does he love the girl so much, then?" said the lady gently.

"Yes; but I am afraid there is no hope for Reddy as long as she thinks there's a chance of her capturing Sylvester."

The lady rose and went to the writing-table. "Would it be any comfort to you, Mr. Woodridge, if you were told that she had not the slightest chance with Sylvester?"

"Yes."

She wrote a few lines on a card, put it in an envelope, and handed it to Woodridge. "Find out where Sylvester is in San Francisco, and give him that card. I think it will satisfy you. And now as I have to catch the return coach in ten minutes, I must ask you to excuse me while I put my things together."

"And you won't first break the news to Reddy for me?"

"No; and I advise you to keep the whole matter to yourself for the present. Goodby!"

She smiled again, fascinatingly as usual, but, as it seemed to him, a trifle wearily, and then passed into the inner room. Years after, in his practical, matter of fact recollections of this strange woman, he always remembered her by this smile.

But she had sufficiently impressed him by her parting adjuration to cause him to answer Reddy's eager inquiries with the statement that Nelly and her mother were greatly preoccupied* with some friends in San Francisco, and to speedily escape further questioning. Reddy's disappointment was somewhat mitigated by the simultaneous announcement of Mrs. Merrydew's departure. But he was still more relieved and gratified to hear, a few days later, of the marriage of Mrs. Merrydew with Louis Sylvester. If, to the general surprise and comment it excited, he contributed only a smile of cynical toleration and superior self-complacency, the reader will understand and not blame him. Nor did the public, who knew the austere completeness of his reform. Nor did Mr. Woodridge, who failed to understand the only actor in this little comedy who might perhaps have differed from them all.

A month later James Reddy married Nelly Woodridge, in the chilly little church at Oakdale. Perhaps by that time it might have occurred to him that although the freshness and fruition of summer were everywhere, the building seemed to be still unwarmed. And when he stepped forth with his bride, and glanced across the prosperous landscape toward the distant bay and headlands of San Francisco, he shivered slightly at the dryly practical kiss of the keen northwestern Trades.

But he was prosperous and comfortable thereafter, as the respectable owner of broad lands and paying shares. It was said that Mrs. Reddy contributed much to the popularity of the hotel by her charming freedom from prejudice and sympathy with mankind; but this was perhaps only due to the contrast to her more serious and at times abstracted husband. At least this was the charitable opinion of the proverbially tolerant and kind-hearted Baroness Streichholzer (*née* Merrydew, and relict of the late lamented Louis Sylvester, Esq.), whom I recently had the pleasure of meeting at Wiesbaden, where the waters and reposeful surroundings strongly reminded her of Oakdale.

THE HEIR OF THE McHULISHES.

I.

THE consul for the United States of America at the port of St. Kentigern was sitting alone in the settled gloom of his private office. Yet it was only high noon, of a "seasonable" winter's day, by the face of the clock that hung like a pallid moon on the murky wall opposite to him. What else could be seen of the apartment by the faint light that struggled through the pall of fog outside the lustreless windows presented the ordinary aspect of a business sanctum. There were a shelf of fog-bound admiralty law, one or two colored prints of ocean steamships under full steam, bow on, tremendously foreshortened, and seeming to force themselves through shadowy partitions; there were engravings of Lincoln and Washington, as unsubstantial and shadowy as the dead themselves. Outside, against the window, which was almost level with the street, an occasional procession of black silhouetted figures of men and women, with prayer-books in their hands and gloom on their faces, seemed to be born of the fog, and prematurely to return to it. At which a conviction of sin overcame the consul. He remembered that it was the Sabbath day, and that he had no business to be at the consulate at all.

Unfortunately, with this shameful conviction came the sound of a bell ringing somewhere in the depths of the building, and the shuffling of feet on the outer steps. The light of his fire had evidently been seen, and like a beacon had attracted some wandering and possibly intoxicated mariner with American papers. The consul walked into the hall with a sudden righteous frigidity of manner. It was one thing to be lounging in one's own office on the Sabbath day, and quite another to be deliberately calling there on business.

He opened the front door, and a middle-aged man entered, accompanying and partly shoving forward a more diffident and younger one. Neither appeared to be a sailor, although both were dressed in that dingy respectability and remoteness of fashion affected by second and third mates when ashore.   They were already well in the hall, and making their way toward the private office, when the elder man said, with an air of casual explanation, "Lookin' for the American consul; I reckon this yer 's the consulate?"

"It is the consulate," said the official dryly, "and I am the consul; but "—

"That 's all right," interrupted the stranger, pushing past him, and opening the door of the private office, into which he shoved his companion.   "Thar now!" he continued to the diffident youth, pointing to a chair, and quite ignoring the presence of the consul ; " thar 's a bit of America. Sit down thar.   You 're under the flag now, and can do as you darn please."   Nevertheless, he looked a little disappointed as he glanced around him, as if he had expected a different environment and possibly a different climate.

"I presume," said the consul suavely, "you wish to see me on some urgent matter; for you probably know that the consulate is closed on Sunday to ordinary business.   I am here myself quite accidentally."

"Then you don't live here?" said the visitor disappointedly.

"No."

"I reckon that's the reason why we did n't see no flag a-flyin' when we was a-huntin' this place yesterday. We were directed here, but I says to Malcolm, says I, 'No; it ain't here, or you'd see the Stars and Stripes afore you'd see anythin' else.' But I reckon you float it over your house, eh?"

The consul here explained smilingly that he did *not* fly a flag over his lodgings, and that except on national holidays it was not customary to display the national ensign on the consulate.

"Then you can't do here — and you a *consul* — what any nigger can do in the States, eh? That's about how it pans out, don't it? But I did n't think *you*'d tumble to it quite so quick, Jack."

At this mention of his Christian name, the consul turned sharply on the speaker. A closer scrutiny of the face before him ended with a flash of reminiscence. The fog without and within seemed to melt away; he was standing once more on a Western hillside with this man; a hundred miles of sparkling sunshine and crisp, dry air stretching around him, and above a blue and arched sky that roofed the third of a continent with six months' summer. And then the fog seemed to come back heavier and thicker to his consciousness. He emotionally stretched out his hand to the stranger. But it was the fog and his personal surroundings which now seemed to be unreal.

"Why it 's Harry Custer!" he said with a laugh that, however, ended in a sigh. "I did n't recognize you in this half light." He then glanced curiously toward the diffident young man, as if to identify another possible old acquaintance.

"Well, I spotted you from the first," said Custer, "though I ain't seen you since we were in Scott's Camp together. That 's ten years ago. You 're lookin' at *him*," he continued, following the consul's wandering eye. "Well, it 's about him that I came to see you. This yer 's a McHulish — a genuine McHulish!"

He paused, as if to give effect to this statement. But the name apparently offered no thrilling suggestion to the consul, who regarded the young man closely for further explanation. He was a fair-faced youth of about twenty years, with pale reddish-brown eyes, dark hair reddish at the roots, and a singular white and pink waxiness of oval cheek, which, however, narrowed suddenly at the angle of the jaw, and fell away with the retreating chin.

"Yes," continued Custer; "I oughter say the *only* McHulish.   He is the direct heir —and of royal descent!   He's one of them McHulishes whose name in them old history times was enough to whoop up the boys and make 'em paint the town red.   A regular campaign boomer — the old McHulish was. Stump speeches and brass-bands warn't in it with the boys when *he* was around. They'd go their bottom dollar and last cartridge — if they'd had cartridges in them days — on him.   That was the regular Mc-Hulish gait.   And Malcolm there's the last of 'em — got the same style of features, too."

Ludicrous as the situation was, it struck the consul dimly, as .through fog and darkness, that the features of the young man were not unfamiliar, and indeed had looked out upon him dimly and vaguely at various times, from various historic canvases.   It was the face of complacent fatuity, incompetency, and inconstancy, which had dragged down strength, competency, and constancy to its own idiotic fate and levels, —a face for whose weaknesses valor and beauty had not only sacrificed themselves, but made things equally unpleasant to a great many minor virtues. Nevertheless, the consul, with an amused sense of its ridiculous incongruity to the grim Scottish Sabbath procession in the street, and the fog-bound volumes of admiralty law in the room, smiled affably.

"Of course our young friend has no desire to test the magic of his name here, in these degenerate days."

"No," said Custer complacently; "though between you and me, old man, there's always no tellin' what might turn up over in this yer monarchy. Things of course are different over our way. But jest now Malcolm will be satisfied to take the title and property to which he's rightful heir."

The consul's face · fell. Alas! it was only the old, old story. Its endless repetitions and variations had been familiar to him even in his youth and in his own land. "Ef that man had his rights," had once been pointed out to him in a wild Western camp, "he'd be now sittin' in scarlet on the right of the Queen of England!" The gentleman who was indicated in this apocalyptical vision, it appeared, simply bore a singular likeness to a reigning Hanoverian family, which for some unexplained reason he had contented himself with bearing with fortitude and patience. But it was in his official capacity that the consul's experience had been the most trying. At times it had seemed to him that much of the real property and peerage of Great Britain was the inherited right of penniless American republicans who had hitherto refrained from presenting their legal claims, and that the habitual first duty of generations of British noblemen on coming into their estates and titles was to ship their heirs and next of kin to America, and then forget all about them. He had listened patiently to claims to positions more or less exalted, — claims often presented with ingenuous sophistry or pathetic simplicity, prosecuted with great good humor, and abandoned with invincible cheerfulness; but they seldom culminated more seriously than in the disbursement of a few dollars by the consul to enable the rightful owner of millions to procure a steerage passage back to his previous democratic retirement. There had been others, less sincere but more pretentious in quality, to whom, however, a letter to the Heralds' College in London was all sufficient, and who, on payment of various fees and emoluments, were enabled to stagger back to New York or Boston with certain unclaimed and forgotten luggage which a more gallant ancestor had scorned to bring with him into the new life, or had thrown aside in his undue haste to make them citizens of the republic. Still, all this had grown monotonous and wearisome, and was disappointing as coming through the intervention of an old friend who ought to know better.

"Of course you have already had legal opinion on the subject over there," said the consul, with a sigh, "but here, you know, you ought first to get some professional advice from those acquainted with Scotch procedure. But perhaps you have that too."

"No," said Custer cheerfully. "Why, it ain't only two months ago that I first saw Malcolm. Tumbled over him on his own farm jest out of MacCorkleville, Kentucky, where he and his fathers before him had been livin' nigh a hundred years — yes, *a hundred years*, by Jove! ever since they first emigrated to the country. Had a talk over it; saw an old Bible about as big and as used up as that," — lifting the well-worn consular Bible, — "with dates in it, and heard the whole story. And here we are."

"And you have consulted no lawyer?" gasped the consul.

"The McHulishes," said an unexpected voice that sounded thin and feminine, "never took any legal decision. From the craggy summits of Glen Crankie he lifted the banner of his forefathers, or raised the war-cry, 'Hulish dhu, ieroe!' from the battlements of Craigiedurrach. And the clan gathered round him with shouts that rent the air. That was the way of it in old times. And the boys whooped him up and stood by him." It was the diffident young man who had half spoken, half recited, with an odd enthusiasm that even the culminating slang could not make conventional.

"That's about the size of it," said Custer, leaning back in his chair easily with an approving glance at the young man. "And I don't know if that ain't the way to work the thing now."

The consul stared hopelessly from the one to the other. It had always seemed possible that this dreadful mania might develop into actual insanity, and he had little doubt but that the younger man's brain was slightly affected. But this did not account for the delusion and expectations of the elder. Harry Custer, as the consul remembered him, was a level-headed, practical miner, whose leaning to adventure and excitement had not prevented him from being a cool speculator, and he had amassed more than a competency by reason of his judicious foresight and prompt action. Yet he was evidently under the glamour of this madman, although outwardly as lazily self-contained as ever.

"Do you mean to tell me," said the consul in a suppressed voice, "that you two have come here equipped only with a statement of facts and a family Bible, and that you expect to take advantage of a feudal enthusiasm which no longer exists — and perhaps never did exist out of the pages of romance — as a means of claiming estates whose titles have long since been settled by law, and can be claimed only under that tenure? Surely I have misunderstood you. You cannot be in earnest."

"Honest Injun," said Custer, nodding his head lazily. "We mean it, but not jest that way you 've put it. F'r instance, it ain't only us two. This yer thing, ole pard, we 're runnin' as a syndicate."

"A syndicate?" echoed the consul.

"A syndicate," repeated Custer. "Half the boys that were at Eagle Camp are in it, and two of Malcolm's neighbors from Kentucky — the regular old Scotch breed like himself; for you know that MacCorkle County was settled by them old Scotch Covenanters, and the folks are Scotch Presbyterians to this day. And for the matter of that, the Eagle boys that are in it are of Scotch descent, or a kind of blend, you know ; in fact, I 'm half Scotch myself — or Irish," he added thoughtfully. "So you see that settles your argument about any local opinion, for if them Scots don't know their own people, who does? "

"May I ask," said the consul, with a desperate attempt to preserve his composure, "what you are proposing to do? "

"Well," said Custer, settling himself comfortably back in his chair again, "that depends. Do you remember the time that we jumped them Mexican claims on the North

Fork — the time them greasers wanted to take in the whole river-bank because they 'd found gold on one of the upper bars? Seems to me we jest went peaceful-like over there one moonshiny night, and took up *their* stakes and set down *ours*. Seems to me *you* were one of the party."

"That was in our own country," returned the consul hastily, "and was an indefensible act, even in a lawless frontier civilization. But you are surely not mad enough even to conceive of such a thing *here!* "

"Keep your hair on, Jack," said Custer lazily. " What 's the matter with constitutional methods, eh? Do you remember the time when we did n't like Pueblo rules, and we laid out Eureka City on their lines, and whooped up the Mexicans and diggers to elect mayor and aldermen, and put the city front on Juanita Creek, and then corraled it for water lots? Seems to me you were county clerk then. Now who 's to keep Dick Macgregor and Joe Hamilton, that are both up the Nile now, from droppin' in over here to see Malcolm in his own house? Who 's goin' to object to Wallace or Baird, who are on this side, doin' the Eytalian lakes, from comin' here on their way home;

or Watson and Moore and Timley, that are livin' over in Paris, from joinin' the boys in givin' Malcolm a housewarmin' in his old home? What's to keep the whole syndicate from gatherin' at Kelpie Island up here off the west coast, among the tombs of Malcolm's ancestors, and fixin' up things generally with the clan?"

"Only one thing," said the consul, with a gravity which he nevertheless felt might be a mistaken attitude. "You should n't have told *me* about it. For if, as your old friend, I cannot keep you from committing an unconceivable folly, as the American consul here it will be my first duty to give notice to our legation, and perhaps warn the authorities. And you may be sure I will do it."

To his surprise Custer leaned forward and pressed his hand with an expression of cheerful relief. "That's so, old pard; I reckoned on it. In fact, I told Malcolm that that would be about your gait. Of course you could n't do otherwise. And it would have been playin' it rather low down on you to have left you out in the cold — without even *that* show in the game. For what you will do in warnin' the other fellows, don't you see, will just waken up the clan. It 's better than a campaign circular."

"Don't be too sure of that," said the consul, with a half-hysterical laugh. "But we won't consider so lamentable a contingency. Come and dine with me, both of you, and we 'll discuss the only thing worth discussing, — your *legal* rights, — and you can tell me your whole story, which, by the way, I have n't heard."

"Sorry, Jack, but it can't be done," said Custer, with his first approach to seriousness of manner. "You see, we 'd made up our mind not to come here again after this first call. We ain't goin' to compromise you."

"I am the best judge of that," returned the consul dryly. Then suddenly changing his manner, he grasped Custer's hands with both his own. "Come, Harry," he said earnestly; "I will not believe that this is not a joke, but I beg of you to promise me one thing, — do not move a step further in this matter without legal counsel. I will give you a letter to a legal friend of mine — a man of affairs, a man of the world, and a Scot as typical, perhaps, as any you have mentioned. State your *legal* case to him — only that; but his opinion will show you also, if I am not mistaken, the folly of your depending upon any sectional or historical sentiment in this matter."

Without waiting for a reply, he sat down and hastily wrote a few lines to a friendly local magnate. When he had handed the note to Custer, the latter looked at the address, and showed it to his young companion.

"Same name, is n't it?" he asked.

"Yes," responded Mr. McHulish.

"Do you know him?" asked the consul, evidently surprised.

"We don't; but he 's a friend of one of the Eagle boys. I reckon we would have seen him anyhow; but we 'll agree with you to hold on until we do. It 's a go. Good-by, old pard! So long."

They both shook the consul's hand, and departed, leaving him staring at the fog into which they had melted as if they were unreal shadows of the past.

II.

The next morning the fog had given way to a palpable, horizontally driving rain, which wet the inside as well as the outside of umbrellas, and caused them to be presented at every conceivable angle as they drifted past the windows of the consulate. There was a tap at the door, and a clerk entered.

"Ye will be in to Sir James MacFen?"

The consul nodded, and added, "Show him in here."

It was the magnate to whom he had sent the note the previous day, a man of large yet slow and cautious nature, learned and even pedantic, yet far-sighted and practical; very human and hearty in social intercourse, which, however, left him as it found him, — with no sentimental or unbusiness-like entanglements. The consul had known him sensible and sturdy at board meetings and executive councils; logical and convincing at political gatherings; decorous and grave in the kirk; and humorous and jovial at festivities, where perhaps later in the evening, in company with others, hands were

clasped over a libation lyrically defined as
a "right guid williewaught." On one of
these occasions they had walked home together, not without some ostentation of
steadiness; yet when MacFen's eminently
respectable front door had closed upon him,
the consul was perfectly satisfied that a distinctly proper and unswerving man of business would issue from it the next morning.

"Ay, but it's a soft day," said Sir James,
removing his gloves. "Ye'll not be gadding
about in this weather."

"You got my note of introduction, I suppose?" said the consul, when the momen-
tous topic of the weather was exhausted.

"Oh, ay."

"And you saw the gentlemen?"

"Ay."

"And what's your opinion of — his
claims?"

"He's a fine lad — that Malcolm — a
fine type of a lad," said Sir James, with an
almost too effusive confidence. "Ye'll be
thinking so yourself — no doubt? Ay,
it's wonderful to consider the preservation
of type so long after its dispersal in other
lands. And it's a strange and wonderful
country that of yours, with its plantations

—as one might say—of homogeneity un-
impaired for so many years, and keeping
the old faith too—and all its strange sur-
vivals. Ay, and that Kentucky, where his
land is—it will be a rich State! It 's
very instructing and interesting to hear his
account of that remarkable region they call
'the blue grass country,' and the stock they
raise there. I 'm obliged to ye, my friend,
for a most edifying and improving evening."

"But his claim—did he not speak of
that?"

"Oh, ay. And that Mr. Custer—he 's
a grand man, and an amusing one. Ye 'll
be great comrades, you and he! Man! it
was delightful to hear him tell of the rare
doings and the bit fun ye two had in the
old times. Eh, sir, but who 'd think that
of the proper American consul at St. Kentigern!" And Sir James leaned back in
his chair, and bestowed an admiring smile
on that official.

The consul thought he began to understand this evasion. "Then you don't think
much of Mr. McHulish's claim?" he said.

"I 'm not saying that."

"But do you really think a claim based

upon a family Bible and a family likeness
a subject for serious consideration?"

"I'm not saying *that* either, laddie."

"Perhaps he has confided to you more
fully than he has to me, or possibly you
yourself knew something in corroboration
of his facts."

"No."

His companion had evidently no desire
to be communicative. But the consul had
heard enough to feel that he was justified
in leaving the matter in his hands. He
had given him fair warning. Yet, nevertheless, he would be even more explicit.

"I do not know," he began, "whether
this young McHulish confided to you his
great reliance upon some peculiar effect of
his presence among the tenants, and of es-
tablishing his claim to the property by ex-
citing the enthusiasm of the clan. It certainly struck me that he had some rather
exaggerated ideas, borrowed, perhaps, from
romances he'd read, like Don Quixote his
books of chivalry. He seems to believe in
the existence of a clan loyalty, and the actual survival of old feudal instincts and of
old feudal methods in the Highlands. He
appears to look upon himself as a kind of

local Prince Charlie, and, by Jove! I 've an idea he 's almost as crazy."

"And why should he na believe in his own kith and kin?" said Sir James, quickly, with a sudden ring in his voice, and a dialectical freedom quite distinct from his former deliberate and cautious utterance. "The McHulishes were chieftains before America was discovered, and many 's the time they overran the border before they went as far as that. If there 's anything in blood and loyalty, it would be strange if they did na respond. And I can tell ye, ma frien', there 's more in the Hielands than any 'romancer,' as ye call them, —ay, even Scott hissel', and he was but an Edinboro' man, — ever dreamed of. Don't fash yoursel' about that. And you and me 'll not agree about Prince Charlie. Some day I 'll tell ye, ma frien', mair aboot that bonnie laddie than ye 'll gather from your partisan historians. Until then ye 'll be wise when ye 'll be talking to Scotchmen not to be expressing your Southern prejudices."

Intensely surprised and amused at this sudden outbreak of enthusiasm on the part of the usually cautious lawyer, the consul could not refrain from accenting it by a marked return to practical business.

"I shall be delighted to learn more about Prince Charlie," he said, smiling, "but just now his prototype — if you 'll allow me to call him so — is a nearer topic, and for the present, at least until he assume his new titles and dignities, has a right to claim my protection, and I am responsible for him as an American citizen. Now, my dear friend, is there really any property, land, or title of any importance involved in his claim, and what and where, in Heaven's name, is it? For I assure you I know nothing practical about it, and cannot make head or tail of it."

Sir James resumed his slow serenity, and gathered up his gloves. "Ay, there 's a great deer-forest in Ballochbrinkie, and there 's part of Loch Phillibeg in Cairngormshire, and there 's Kelpie Island off Moreovershire. Ay, there 's enough land when the crofters are cleared off, and the small sheep-tenants evicted. It will be a grand property then."

The consul stared. "The crofters and tenants evicted!" he repeated. "Are they not part of the clan, and loyal to the McHulish?"

"The McHulish," said Sir James with great deliberation, "has n't set foot there for years. They 'd be burning him in effigy."

"But," said the astonished consul, "that 's rather bad for the expectant heir — and the magic of the McHulish presence."

" I 'm not saying that," returned Sir James cautiously. "Ye see he can be making better arrangements with the family on account of it."

"With the family? " repeated the consul. "Then does he talk of compromising? "

"I mean they would be more likely to sell for a fair consideration, and he 'd be better paying money to them than the lawyers. The syndicate will be rich, eh? And I 'm not saying the McHulish would n't take Kentucky lands in exchange. It 's a fine country, that blue grass district."

The consul stared at Sir James so long that a faint smile came into the latter's shrewd eyes; at which the consul smiled, too. A vague air of relief and understanding seemed to fill the apartment.

" Oh, ay," continued Sir James, drawing on his gloves with easy deliberation, "he 's a fine lad that Malcolm, and it 's a praiseworthy instinct in him to wish to return to the land of his forebears, and take his place again among them. And I 'm noticing, Mr. Consul, that a great many of your countrymen are doing the same. Eh, yours is a gran' country of progress and ceevel and religious liberty, but for a' that, as Burns says, it 's in your blood to turn to the auld home again. And it 's a fine thing to have the money to do it —and, I 'm thinking, money well spent all around. Good - morning. Eh, but I 'm forgetting that I wanted to ask you to dine with me and Malcolm, and your Mr. Custer, and Mr. Watson, who will be one of your syndicate, and whom I once met abroad. But ye 'll get a bit note of invitation, with the day, from me later."

The consul remembered that Custer had said that one of the "Eagle boys" had known Sir James. This was evidently Watson. He smiled again, but this time Sir James responded only in a general sort of way, as he genially bowed himself out of the room.

The consul watched his solid and eminently respectable figure as it passed the window, and then returned to his desk,

still smiling.   First of all he was relieved.
What had seemed to him a wild and reckless enterprise, with possibly some grim
international complications on the part of
his compatriots, had simply resolved itself
into an ordinary business speculation — the
ethics of which they had pretty equally
divided with the local operators.   If anything, it seemed that the Scotchman would
get the best of the bargain, and that, for
once at least, his countrymen were deficient
in foresight.   But that was a matter between the parties, and Custer himself would
probably be the first to resent any suggestion of the kind from the consul.   The
vision of the McHulish burned in effigy by
his devoted tenants and retainers, and the
thought that the prosaic dollars of his countrymen would be substituted for the potent
presence of the heir, tickled, it is to be
feared, the saturnine humor of the consul.
He had taken an invincible dislike to the
callow representative of the McHulish, who
he felt had in some extraordinary way imposed upon Custer's credulity.   But then
he had apparently imposed equally upon
the practical Sir James.   The thought of
this sham ideal of feudal and privileged

incompetency being elevated to actual position by the combined efforts of American
republicans and hard-headed Scotch dissen-
ters, on whom the soft Scotch mists fell
from above with equal impartiality, struck
him as being very amusing, and for some
time thereafter lightened the respectable
gloom of his office. Other engagements
prevented his attendance at Sir James's
dinner, although he was informed afterward
that it had passed off with great *éclat*, the
later singing of "Auld lang Syne," and the
drinking of the health of Custer and Malcolm with "Hieland honors." He learned
also that Sir James had invited Custer and
Malcolm to his lacustrine country-seat in
the early spring. But he learned nothing
more of the progress of Malcolm's claim,
its details, or the manner in which it was
prosecuted. No one else seemed to know
anything about it; it found no echo in the
gossip of the clubs, or in the newspapers of
St. Kentigern. In the absence of the parties connected with it, it began to assume
to him the aspect of a half-humorous romance. He often found himself wondering
if there had been any other purpose in this
quest or speculation than what had ap-

peared on the surface, it seemed so inadequate in result. It would have been so
perfectly . easy for a wealthy syndicate to
buy up a much more valuable estate. He
disbelieved utterly in the sincerity of Malcolm's sentimental attitude. There must
be some other reason — perhaps not known
even to the syndicate.

One day he thought that he had found it.
He had received a note addressed from one
of the principal hotels, but bearing a large
personal crest on paper and envelope. A
Miss Kirkby, passing through St. Kentigern on her way to Edinburgh, desired to
see the consul the next day, if he would
appoint an hour at the consulate; or, as her
time was limited, she would take it as a
great favor if he would call at her hotel.
Although a countrywoman, her name might
not be so well known to him as those of her
"old friends" Harry Custer, Esq., and Sir
Malcolm McHulish. The consul was a little surprised; the use of the title — unless
it referred to some other McHulish — would
seem to indicate that Malcolm's claim was
successful. He had, however, no previous
knowledge of the title of "Sir" in connection with the estate, and it was probable

that his fair correspondent — like most of her countrywomen — was more appreciative than correct in her bestowal of dignities. He determined to waive his ordinary business rules, and to call upon her at once, accepting, as became his patriotism, that charming tyranny which the American woman usually reserves exclusively for her devoted countrymen.

She received him with an affectation of patronage, as if she had lately become uneasily conscious of being in a country where there were distinctions of class. She was young, pretty, and tastefully dressed; the national feminine adaptability had not, however, extended to her voice and accent. Both were strongly Southwestern, and as she began to speak she seemed to lose her momentary affectation.

"It was mighty good of you to come and see me, for the fact is, I did n't admire going to your consulate — not one bit. You see, I 'm a Southern girl, and never was 'reconstructed' either. I don't hanker after your Gov'ment. I have n't recognized it, and don't want to. I reckon I ain't been under the flag since the wah. So you see, I have n't any papers to get authenticated, nor any certificates to ask for, and ain't wanting any advice or protection. I thought I 'd be fair and square with you from the word 'go.' "

Nothing could be more fascinating and infectious than the mirthful ingenuousness which accompanied and seemed to mitigate this ungracious speech, and the consul was greatly amused, albeit conscious that it was only an attitude, and perhaps somewhat worn in sentiment. He knew that during the war of the rebellion, and directly after it, Great Britain was the resort of certain Americans from the West as well as from the South who sought social distinction by the affectation of dissatisfaction with their own government or the ostentatious simulation of enforced exile; but he was quite unprepared for this senseless protraction of dead and gone issues. He ventured to point out with good-humored practicality that several years had elapsed since the war, that the South and North were honorably reconciled, and that he was legally supposed to represent Kentucky as well as New York. "Your friends," he added smilingly, "Mr. Custer and Mr. McHulish, seemed to accept the fact without any posthumous sentiment."

"I don't go much on that," she said with a laugh. "I've been living in Paris till maw — who's lying down upstairs — came over and brought me across to England for a look around. And I reckon Malcolm's got to keep touch with you on account of his property."

The consul smiled. "Ah, then, I hope you can tell me something about *that*, for I really don't know whether he has established his claim or not."

"Why," returned the girl with naïve astonishment, "that was just what I was going to ask *you*. He reckoned you'd know all about it."

"I haven't heard anything of the claim for two months," said the consul; "but from your reference to him as 'Sir Malcolm,' I presumed you considered it settled. Though, of course, even then he wouldn't be 'Sir Malcolm,' and you might have meant somebody else."

"Well, then, Lord Malcolm — I can't get the hang of those titles yet."

"Neither 'Lord' nor 'Sir'; you know the estate carries no title whatever with it," said the consul smilingly.

"But wouldn't he be the laird of something or other, you know?"

"Yes; but that is only a Scotch description, not a title. It's not the same as Lord."

The young girl looked at him with undisguised astonishment. A half laugh twitched the corners of her mouth. "Are you sure?" she said.

"Perfectly," returned the consul, a little impatiently; "but do I understand that you really know nothing more of the progress of the claim?"

Miss Kirkby, still abstracted by some humorous astonishment, said quickly: "Wait a minute. I'll just run up and see if maw's coming down. She'd admire to see you." Then she stopped, hesitated, and as she rose added, "Then a laird's wife wouldn't be Lady anything, anyway, would she?"

"She certainly would acquire no title merely through her marriage."

The young girl laughed again, nodded, and disappeared. The consul, amused yet somewhat perplexed over the naïve brusqueness of the interview, waited patiently. Presently she returned, a little out of breath, but apparently still enjoying some facetious retrospect, and said, "Maw will be down soon."   After a pause, fixing her bright eyes mischievously on the consul, she continued: —

"Did you see much of Malcolm?"

"I saw him only once."

"What did you think of him?"

The consul in so brief a period had been unable to judge.

"You would n't think I was half engaged to him, would you?"

The consul was obliged again to protest that in so short an interview he had been unable to conceive of Malcolm's good fortune.

"I know what you mean," said the girl lightly. "You think he 's a crank. But it 's all over now; the engagement 's off."

"I trust that this does not mean that you doubt his success?"

The lady shrugged her shoulders disdainfully. "That 's all right enough, I reckon. There 's a hundred thousand dollars in the syndicate. Maw put in twenty thousand, and Custer 's bound to make it go — particularly as there 's some talk of a compromise. But Malcolm 's a crank, and I reckon if it was n't for the compromise the syndicate would n't have much show. Why,

he did n't even know that the McHulishes
had no title."

"Do you think he has been suffering
under a delusion in regard to his relationship?"

"No; he was only a fool in the way he
wanted to prove it. He actually got these
boys to think it could be filibustered into
his possession. Had a sort of idea of 'a
rising in the Highlands,' you know, like
that poem or picture — which is it? And
those fool boys, and Custer among them,
thought it would be great fun and a great
spree. Luckily, maw had the gumption to
get Watson to write over about it to one of
his friends, a Mr. — Mr. — MacFen, a very
prominent man."

"Perhaps you mean Sir James MacFen,"
suggested the consul. "He 's a knight.
And what did *he* say?" he added eagerly.

"Oh, he wrote a most sensible letter,"
returned the lady, apparently mollified by
the title of Watson's adviser, "saying that
there was little doubt, if any, that if the
American McHulishes wanted the old estate
they could get it by the expenditure of a little capital. He offered to make the trial;
that was the compromise they 're talking

about.   But he did n't say anything about there being no 'Lord' McHulish."

"Perhaps he thought, as you were Americans, you did n't care for *that*," said the consul dryly.

"That's no reason why we should n't have it if it belonged to us, or we chose to pay for it," said the lady pertly.

"Then your changed personal relations with Mr. McHulish is the reason why you hear so little of his progress or his expectations?"

"Yes; but he don't know that they are changed, for we have n't seen him since we 've been here, although they say he 's here, and hiding somewhere about."

" Why should he be hiding?"

The young girl lifted her pretty brows. "Maybe he thinks it 's mysterious.   Did n't I tell you he was a crank?"   Yet she laughed so naïvely, and with such sublime unconsciousness of any reflection on herself, that the consul was obliged to smile too.

"You certainly do not seem to be breaking your heart as well as your engagement," he said.

" Not much — but here comes maw. Look here," she said, turning suddenly and coaxingly upon him, "if she asks you to come along with us up north, you 'll come, won't you? Do! It will be such fun!"

"Up north?" repeated the consul interrogatively.

" Yes ; to see the property. Here 's maw."

A more languid but equally well - appointed woman had entered the room. When the ceremony of introduction was over, she turned to her daughter and said, "Run away, dear, while I talk business with — er — this gentleman," and, as the girl withdrew laughingly, she half stifled a reminiscent yawn, and raised her heavy lids to the consul.

"You 've had a talk with my Elsie?"

The consul confessed to having had that pleasure.

" She speaks her mind," said Mrs. Kirkby wearily, "but she means well, and for all her flightiness her head 's level. And since her father died she runs me," she continued with a slight laugh. After a pause, she added abstractedly, "I suppose she told you of her engagement to young . McHulish?"

"Yes; but she said she had broken it."

Mrs. Kirkby lifted her eyebrows with an expression of relief. "It was a piece of girl and boy foolishness, anyway," she said. "Elsie and he were children together at MacCorkleville, — second cousins, in fact, — and I reckon he got her fancy excited over his nobility, and his being the chief of the McHulishes. Of course Custer will manage to get something for the shareholders out of it, — I never knew him to fail in a money speculation yet, — but I think that's about all. I had an idea of going up with Elsie to take a look at the property, and I thought of asking you to join us. Did Elsie tell you? I know she'd like it — and so would I."

For all her indolent, purposeless manner, there was enough latent sincerity and earnestness in her request to interest the consul. Besides, his own curiosity in regard to this singularly supported claim was excited, and here seemed to be an opportunity of satisfying it. He was not quite sure, either, that his previous antagonism to his fair countrywoman's apparent selfishness and snobbery was entirely just. He had been absent from America a long time; perhaps it was he himself who had changed, and lost touch with his compatriots. And yet the demonstrative independence and recklessness of men like Custer were less objectionable to, and less inconsistent with, his American ideas than the snobbishness and almost servile adaptability of the women. Or was it possible that it was only a weakness of the sex, which no republican nativity or education could eliminate? Nevertheless he looked up smilingly.

"But the property is, I understand, scattered about in various places," he said.

"Oh, but we mean to go only to Kelpie Island, where there is the ruin of an old castle. Elsie must see that."

The consul thought it might be amusing. "By all means let us see that. I shall be delighted to go with you."

His ready and unqualified assent appeared to relieve and dissipate the lady's abstraction. She became more natural and confiding; spoke freely of Malcolm's mania, which she seemed to accept as a hallucination or a conviction with equal cheerfulness, and, in brief, convinced the consul that her connection with the scheme was only the caprice of inexperienced and unaccustomed idleness. He left her, promising to return the next day and arrange for their early departure.

His way home lay through one of the public squares of St. Kentigern, at an hour of the afternoon when it was crossed by working men and women returning to their quarters from the docks and factories. Never in any light a picturesque or even cheery procession, there were days when its unwholesome, monotonous poverty and dull hopelessness of prospect impressed him more forcibly. He remembered how at first the spectacle of barefooted girls and women slipping through fog and mist across the greasy pavement had offended his fresh New World conception of a more tenderly nurtured sex, until his susceptibilities seemed to have grown as callous and hardened as the flesh he looked upon, and he had begun to regard them from the easy local standpoint of a distinct and differently equipped class.

It chanced, also, that this afternoon some of the male workers had added to their usual solidity a singular trance-like intoxication. It had often struck him before as a form of drunkenness peculiar to the St. Kentigern laborers. Men passed him

singly and silently, as if following some
vague alcoholic dream, or moving through
some Scotch mist of whiskey and water.
Others clung unsteadily but as silently together, with no trace of convivial fellow-
ship or hilarity in their dull fixed features
and mechanically moving limbs. There
was something weird in this mirthless companionship, and the appalling loneliness of
those fixed or abstracted eyes. Suddenly
he was aware of two men who were reeling
toward him under the influence of this
drug-like intoxication, and he was startled
by a likeness which one of them bore to
some one he had seen; but where, and under what circumstances, he could not deter-
mine. The fatuous eye, the features of
complacent vanity and self-satisfied reverie
were there, either intensified by drink, or
perhaps suggesting it through some other
equally hopeless form of hallucination. He
turned and followed the man, trying to
identify him through his companion, who
appeared to be a petty tradesman of a
shrewder, more material type. But in
vain, and as the pair turned into a side
street the consul slowly retraced his steps.
But he had not proceeded far before the

recollection that had escaped him returned, and he knew that the likeness suggested by the face he had seen was that of Malcolm McHulish.

III.

A journey to Kelpie Island consisted of a series of consecutive episodes by rail, by coach, and by steamboat. The consul was already familiar with them, as indeed were most of the civilized world, for it seemed that all roads at certain seasons led out of and returned to St. Kentigern as a point in a vast circle wherein travelers were sure to meet one another again, coming or going, at certain depots and caravansáries with more or less superiority or envy. Tourists on the road to the historic crags of Wateffa came sharply upon other tourists returning from them, and glared suspiciously at them, as if to wrest the dread secret from their souls — a scrutiny which the others returned with half-humorous pity or superior calm.

The consul knew, also, that the service by boat and rail was admirable and skillful; for were not the righteous St. Kentigerners of the tribe of Tubal-cain, great artificers in steel and iron, and a mighty race of en-

gineers before the Lord, who had carried
their calling and accent beyond the seas?
He knew, too, that the land of these delightful caravansaries overflowed with mar-
malade and honey, and that the manna of
delicious scones and cakes fell even upon
deserted waters of crag and heather.   He
knew that their way would lie through
much scenery whose rude barrenness, and
grim economy of vegetation, had been
usually accepted by cockney tourists for
sublimity and grandeur; but he knew, also,
that its severity was mitigated by lowland
glimpses of sylvan luxuriance and tangled
delicacy utterly unlike the complacent snug-
ness of an English pastoral landscape, with
which it was often confounded and misunderstood, as being tame and civilized.

It rained the day they left St. Kentigern,
and the next, and the day after that, spas-
modically, as regarded local effort, sporadi-
cally, as seen through the filmed windows
of railway carriages or from the shining
decks of steamboats.   There was always a
shower being sown somewhere along the
valley, or reluctantly tearing itself from a
mountain-top, or being pulled into long
threads from the leaden bosom of a lake;

the coach swept in and out of them to the folding and unfolding of umbrellas and mackintoshes, accompanied by flying beams of sunlight that raced with the vehicle on long hillsides, and vanished at the turn of the road. There were hat-lifting scurries of wind down the mountain-side, small tumults in little lakes below, hysteric ebullitions on mild, melancholy inland seas, boisterous passages of nearly half an hour with landings on tempestuous miniature quays. All this seen through wonderful aqueous vapor, against a background of sky darkened at times to the depths of an India ink washed sketch, but more usually blurred and confused on the surface like the gray silhouette of a child's slate-pencil drawing, half rubbed from the slate by soft palms. Occasionally a rare glinting of real sunshine on a distant fringe of dripping larches made some frowning crest appear to smile as through wet lashes.

Miss Elsie tucked her little feet under the mackintosh. "I know," she said sadly, "I should get web-footed if I stayed here long. Why, it's like coming down from Ararat just after the deluge cleared up."

Mrs. Kirkby suggested that if the sun

would only shine squarely and decently, like a Christian, for a few moments, they could see the prospect better.

The consul here pointed out that the admirers of Scotch scenery thought that this was its greatest charm. It was this misty effect which made it so superior to what they called the vulgar chromos and sun-pictures of less favored lands.

"You mean because it prevents folks from seeing how poor the view really is."

The consul remarked that perhaps distance was lacking. As to the sun shining in a Christian way, this might depend upon the local idea of Christianity.

"Well, I don't call the scenery giddy or frivolous, certainly. And I reckon I begin to understand the kind of sermons Malcolm's folks brought over to MacCorkleville. I guess they did n't know much of the heaven they only saw once a year. Why, even the highest hills — which they call mountains here — ain't big enough to get above the fogs of their own creating."

Feminine wit is not apt to be abstract. It struck the consul that in Miss Elsie's sprightliness there was the usual ulterior and personal object, and he glanced around at his fellow-passengers. The object evidently was sitting at the end of the opposite seat, an amused but well-behaved listener. For the rest, he was still young and reserved, but in face, figure, and dress utterly unlike his companions, — an Englishman of a pronounced and distinct type, the man of society and clubs. While there was more or less hinting of local influence in the apparel of the others, — there was a kilt, and bare, unweather-beaten knees from Birmingham, and even the American Elsie wore a bewitching tam-o'-shanter, — the stranger carried easy distinction, from his tweed traveling-cap to his well-made shoes and gaiters, as an unmistakable Southerner. His deep and pleasantly level voice had been heard only once or twice, and then only in answering questions, and his quiet, composed eyes alone had responded to the young girl's provocation.

They were passing a brown glen, in the cheerless depths of which a brown watercourse, a shade lighter, was running, and occasionally foaming like brown beer. Beyond it heaved an arid bulk of hillside, the scant vegetation of which, scattered like patches of hair, made it look like the decaying hide of some huge antediluvian ruminant. On the dreariest part of the dreary slope rose the ruins of a tower, and crumbling walls and battlements.

"Whatever possessed folks to build there?" said Miss Elsie. "If they were poor, it might be some excuse; but that those old swells, or chiefs, should put up a castle in such a God-forsaken place gets *me*."

"But don't you know, they *were* poor, according to our modern ideas, and I fancy they built these things more for defense than show, and really more to gather in cattle — like one of your Texan ranches — after a raid. That is, I have heard so; I rather fancy that was the idea, was n't it?" It was the Englishman who had spoken, and was now looking around at the other passengers as if in easy deference to local opinion.

"What raid?" said Miss Elsie, animatedly. "Oh, yes; I see — one of their old border raids — moss-troopers. I used to like to read about them."

"I fancy, don't you know," said the Englishman slowly, "that it was n't exactly *that* sort of thing, you know, for it 's a good way from the border; but it was one of their raids upon their neighbors, to lift their cattle — steal 'em, in fact. That 's the way those chaps had. But of course you 've read all about that. You Americans, don't you know, are all up in these historical matters."

"Eh, but they were often reprisals," said a Scotch passenger.

"I don't suppose they took much trouble to inquire if the beasts belonged to an enemy," said the Englishman.

But here Miss Elsie spoke of castles generally, and averred that the dearest wish of her life was to see Macbeth's castle at Glamis, where Duncan was murdered. At which the Englishman, still deferentially, mistrusted the fact that the murder had been committed there, and thought that the castle to which Shakespeare probably referred, if he had n't invented the murder, too, was farther north, at Cawdor. "You know," he added playfully, "over there in America you 've discovered that Shakespeare himself was an invention."

This led to some retaliating brilliancy from the young lady, and when the coach stopped at the next station their conversation had presumably become interesting enough to justify him in securing a seat nearer to her.   The talk returning to ruins, Miss Elsie informed him that they were going to see some on Kelpie Island.   The consul, from some instinctive impulse, — perhaps a recollection of Custer's peculiar methods, — gave her a sign of warning. But the Englishman only lifted his eyebrows in a kind of half-humorous concern.

"I don't think you'd like it, you know. It's a beastly place, — rocks and sea, — worse than this, and half the time you can't see the mainland, only a mile away. Really, you know, they ought n't to have induced you to take tickets there — those excursion - ticket chaps.   They 're jolly frauds.   It 's no place for a stranger to go to."

"But there are the ruins of an old castle, the old seat of " — began the astonished Miss Elsie; but she was again stopped by a significant glance from the consul.

"I believe there was something of the kind there once — something like your friends the cattle-stealers' castle over on that hillside," returned the Englishman; "but the stones were taken by the fishermen for their cabins, and the walls were quite pulled down."

"How dared they do that?" said the young lady indignantly. "I call it not only sacrilege, but stealing."

"It was defrauding the owner of the property; they might as well take his money," said Mrs. Kirkby, in languid protest.

The smile which this outburst of proprietorial indignation brought to the face of the consul lingered with the Englishman's reply.

"But it was only robbing the old robbers, don't you know, and they put their spoils to better use than their old masters did; certainly to more practical use than the owners do now, for the ruins are good for nothing."

"But the hallowed associations — the picturesqueness!" continued Mrs. Kirkby, with languid interest.

"The associations wouldn't be anything except to the family, you know; and I should fancy they wouldn't be either hallowed or pleasant. As for picturesqueness, the ruins are beastly ugly; weather-beaten instead of being mellowed by time, you know, and bare where they ought to be hid-

den by vines and moss. I can't make out
why anybody sent you there, for you Americans are rather particular about your sight-
seeing."

"We heard of them through a friend,"
said the consul, with assumed carelessness.
"Perhaps it's as good an excuse as any for
a pleasant journey."

"And very likely your friend mistook
it for something else, or was himself imposed upon," said the Englishman politely.
"But you might not think it so, and, after
all," he added thoughtfully, "it's years
since I've seen it. I only meant that I
could show you something better a few
miles from my place in Gloucestershire,
and not quite so far from a railway as this.
If," he added with a pleasant deliberation
which was the real courtesy of his conventionally worded speech, "you ever happened
at any time to be anywhere near Audrey
Edge, and would look me up, I should be
glad to show it to you and your friends."
An hour later, when he left them at a railway station where their paths diverged,
Miss Elsie recovered a fluency that she had
lately checked. "Well, I like that! He
never told us his name, or offered a card. I

wonder if they call that an invitation over here. Does he suppose anybody 's going to look up his old Audrey Edge — perhaps it 's named after his wife — to find out who *he* is? He might have been civil enough to have left his name, if he — meant anything."

"But I assure you he was perfectly sincere, and meant an invitation," returned the consul smilingly. "Audrey Edge is evidently a well-known place, and he a man of some position. That is why he did n't specify either."

"Well, you won't catch me going there," said Miss Elsie.

"You would be quite right in either going or staying away," said the consul simply.

Miss Elsie tossed her head slightly. Nevertheless, before they left the station, she informed him that she had been told that the station-master had addressed the stranger as "my lord," and that another passenger had said he was "Lord Duncaster."

"And that proves " —

"That I 'm right," said the young lady decisively, "and that his invitation was a mere form."

It was after sundown when they reached

the picturesque and well-appointed hotel that lifted itself above the little fishing-village which fronted Kelpie Island. The hotel was in as strong contrast to the narrow, curving street of dull, comfortless-looking stone cottages below it, as were the smart tourists who had just landed from the steamer to the hard-visaged, roughly clad villagers who watched them with a certain mingling of critical independence and superior self - righteousness. As the new arrivals walked down the main street, half beach, half thoroughfare, their baggage following them in low trolleys drawn by porters at their heels, like a decorous funeral, the joyless faces of the lookers-on added to the resemblance. Beyond them, in the prolonged northern twilight, the waters of the bay took on a peculiar pewtery brightness, but with the usual mourning-edged border of Scotch seacoast scenery. Low banks of cloud lay on the chill sea; the outlines of Kelpie Island were hidden.

But the interior of the hotel, bright with the latest fastidiousness in modern decoration and art-furniture, and gay with pictured canvases and color, seemed to mock the sullen landscape, and the sterile crags amid which the building was set. An attempt to make a pleasance in this barren waste had resulted only in empty vases, bleak statuary, and iron settees, as cold and slippery to the touch as the sides of their steamer.

"It 'll be a fine morning to-morra, and ther 'll be a boat going away to Kelpie for a peekneek in the ruins," said the porter, as the consul and his fair companions looked doubtfully from the windows of the cheerful hall.

A picnic in the sacred ruins of Kelpie! The consul saw the ladies stiffening with indignation at this trespass upon their possible rights and probable privileges, and glanced at them warningly.

"Do you mean to say that it is common property, and *anybody* can go there?" demanded Miss Elsie scornfully.

"No; it 's only the hotel that owns the boat and gives the tickets — a half-crown the passage."

"And do the owners, the McHulishes, permit this?"

The porter looked at them with a puzzled, half - pitying politeness. He was a handsome, tall, broad-shouldered young fellow, with a certain naïve and gentle courtesy of manner that relieved his strong accent. "Oh, ay," he said, with a reassuring smile; "ye 'll no be troubled by *them*. I 'll just gang away noo, and see if I can secure the teekets."

An elderly guest, who was examining a time-table on the wall, turned to them as the porter disappeared.

"Ye 'll be strangers noo, and not knowing that Tonalt the porter is a McHulish hissel'?" he said deliberately.

"A what?" said the astonished Miss Elsie.

"A McHulish. Ay, one of the family. The McHulishes of Kelpie were his own forebears. Eh, but he 's a fine lad, and doin' well for the hotel."

Miss Elsie extinguished a sudden smile with her handkerchief as her mother anxiously inquired, "And are the family as poor as that?"

"But I am not saying he 's *poor*, ma'am, no," replied the stranger, with native caution. "What wi' tips and gratooities and percentages on the teekets, it 's a bit of money he 'll be having in the bank noo."

The prophecy of Donald McHulish as to the weather came true. The next morning was bright and sunny, and the boat to Kelpie Island — a large yawl — duly received its complement of passengers and provision hampers. The ladies had apparently become more tolerant of their fellow pleasure-seekers, and it appeared that Miss Elsie had even overcome her hilarity at the discovery of what "might have been" a relative in the person of the porter Donald. "I had a long talk with him before breakfast this morning," she said gayly, "and I know all about him. It appears that there are hundreds of him — all McHulishes — all along the coast and elsewhere — only none of them ever lived *on* the island, and don't want to. But he looks more like a 'laird' and a chief than Malcolm, and if it comes to choosing a head of the family, remember, maw, I shall vote solid for him."

"How can you go on so, Elsie?" said Mrs. Kirkby, with languid protest. "Only I trust you did n't say anything to him of the syndicate. And, thank Heaven! the property is n't here."

"No; the waiter tells me all the lovely things we had for breakfast came from miles away. And they don't seem to have ever raised anything on the island, from its looks. Think of having to row three miles for the morning's milk!"

There was certainly very little appearance of vegetation on the sterile crags that soon began to lift themselves above the steely waves ahead. A few scraggy trees and bushes, which twisted and writhed like vines around the square tower and crumbling walls of an irregular but angular building, looked in their brown shadows like part of the débris.

"It's just like a burnt-down bone-boiling factory," said Miss Elsie critically; " and I should n't wonder if that really was old McHulish's business. They could n't have it on the mainland for its being a nuisance."

Nevertheless, she was one of the first to leap ashore when the yawl's bow grated in a pebbly cove, and carried her pretty but incongruous little slippers through the seaweed, wet sand, and slimy cobbles with a heroism that redeemed her vanity. A scrambling ascent of a few moments brought them to a wall with a gap in it, which gave easy ingress to the interior of the ruins. This was merely a little curving hollow from which the outlines of the plan had long since faded. It was kept green by the brown walls, which, like the crags of the mainland valleys, sheltered it from the incessant strife of the Atlantic gales. A few pale flowers that might have grown in a damp cellar shivered against the stones. Scraps of newspapers, soda-water and beer bottles, highly decorated old provision tins, and spent cartridge cases, — the remains of chilly picnics and damp shooting luncheons, — had at first sight lent color to the foreground by mere contrast, but the corrosion of time and weather had blackened rather than mellowed the walls in a way which forcibly reminded the consul of Miss Elsie's simile of the "burnt - down factory." The view from the square tower — a mere roost for unclean sea-fowl, from the sides of which rags of peeling moss and vine hung like tattered clothing — was equally depressing. The few fishermen's huts along the shore were built of stones taken from the ruin, and roofed in with sodden beams and timbers in the last stages of deliquescence. The thick smoke of smouldering peat-fires came from the low chimneys, and drifted across the ruins with the odors of drying fish.

"I've just seen a sort of ground-plan of the castle," said Miss Elsie cheerfully. "It never had a room in it as big as our bedroom in the hotel, and there were n't windows enough to go round. A slit in the wall, about two inches wide by two feet long, was considered dazzling extravagance to Malcolm's ancestors. I don't wonder some of 'em broke out and swam over to America. That reminds me. Who do you suppose is here — came over from the hotel in a boat of his own, just to see maw!"

"Not Malcolm, surely."

"Not much," replied Miss Elsie, setting her small lips together. "It 's Mr. Custer. He 's talking business with her now down on the beach. They 'll be here when lunch is ready."

The consul remembered the romantic plan which the enthusiastic Custer had imparted to him in the foggy consulate at St. Kentigern, and then thought of the matter of fact tourists, the few stolid fishermen, and the prosaic ruins around them, and smiled. He looked up, and saw that Miss Elsie was watching him.

"You know Mr. Custer, don't you?"

"We are old Californian friends."

"I thought so; but I think he looked a little upset when he heard you were here, too."

He certainly was a little awkward, as if struggling with some half-humorous embarrassment, as he came forward a few moments later with Mrs. Kirkby. But the stimulation of the keen sea air triumphed over the infelicities of the situation and surroundings, and the little party were presently enjoying their well-selected luncheon with the wholesome appetite of travel and change. The chill damp made limp the napkins and table-cloth, and invaded the victuals; the wind, which was rising, whistled round the walls, and made miniature cyclones of the torn paper and dried twigs around them: but they ate, drank, and were merry. At the end of the repast the two gentlemen rose to light their cigars in the lee of the wall.

"I suppose you know all about Malcolm?" said Custer, after an awkward pause.

"My dear fellow," said the consul, somewhat impatiently, "I know nothing about him, and you ought to know that by this time."

"I thought *your friend*, Sir James, might have told you," continued Custer, with significant emphasis.

"I have not seen Sir James for two months."

"Well, Malcolm 's a crank — always was one, I reckon, and is reg'larly off his head now. Yes, sir; Scotch whiskey and your friend Sir James finished him. After that dinner at MacFen's he was done for — went wild. Danced a sword-dance, or a strathspey, or some other blamed thing, on the table, and yelled louder than the pipes. So they all did. Jack, I 've painted the town red once myself; I thought I knew what a first-class jamboree was: but they were prayer-meetings to that show. Everybody was blind drunk — but they all got over it except *him*. *They* were a different lot of men the next day, as cool and cautious as you please, but *he* was shut up for a week, and came out crazy."

"But what 's that to do with his claim?"

"Well, there ain't much use 'whooping up the boys' when only the whooper gets wild."

"Still, that does not affect any right he may have in the property."

"But it affects the syndicate," said Custer gloomily; "and when we found that he
was whooping up some shopkeepers and
factory hands who claimed to belong to the
clan, — and you can't heave a stone at a
dog around here without hitting a McHulish, — we concluded we had n't much use
for him ornamentally. So we shipped him
home last steamer."

"And the property?"

"Oh, that's all right," said Custer, still
gloomily. "We 've effected an amicable
compromise, as Sir James calls it. That
means we 've taken a lot of land somewhere
north, that you can shoot over — that is,
you need n't be afraid of hitting a house,
or a tree, or a man anywhere; and we 've
got a strip more of the same sort on the
seashore somewhere off here, occupied only
by some gay galoots called crofters, and
you can raise a lawsuit and an imprecation
on every acre. Then there 's this soul-
subduing, sequestered spot, and what 's left
of the old bone-boiling establishment, and
the rights of fishing and peat-burning, and
otherwise creating a nuisance off the mainland. It cost the syndicate only a hundred
thousand dollars, half cash and half in

Texan and Kentucky grass lands. But we 've carried the thing through."

"I congratulate you," said the consul.

"Thanks." Custer puffed at his cigar for a few moments. "That Sir James MacFen is a fine man."

"He is."

"A large, broad, all-round man. Knows everything and everybody, don't he?"

"I think so."

"Big man in the church, I should say? No slouch at a party canvass, or ward politics, eh? As a board director, or president, just takes the cake, don't he?"

"I believe so."

"Nothing mean about Jimmy as an advocate or an arbitrator, either, is there? Rings the bell every time, don't he? Financiers take a back seat when he 's around? Owns half of Scotland by this time, I reckon."

The consul believed that Sir James had the reputation of being exceedingly sagacious in financial and mercantile matters, and that he was a man of some wealth.

"Naturally. I wonder what he 'd take to come over to America, and give the boys points," continued Custer, in meditative admiration. "There were two or three men on Scott's River, and one Chinaman, that we used to think smart, but they were doddering ijuts to *him*. And as for me — I say, Jack, you did n't see any hayseed in my hair that day I walked inter your consulate, did you?"

The consul smilingly admitted that he had not noticed these signs of rustic innocence in his friend.

"Nor any flies? Well, for all that, when I get home I 'm going to resign. No more foreign investments for *me*. When anybody calls at the consulate and asks for H. J. Custer, say you don't know me. And you don't. And I say, Jack, try to smooth things over for me with *her*."

"With Miss Elsie?"

Custer cast a glance of profound pity upon the consul. "No; with Mrs. Kirkby, of course. See?"

The consul thought he did see, and that he had at last found a clue to Custer's extraordinary speculation. But, like most theorists who argue from a single fact, a few months later he might have doubted his deduction.

He was staying at a large country-house

many miles distant from the scene of his late experiences. Already they had faded from his memory with the departure of his compatriots from St. Kentigern. He was smoking by the fire in the billiard-room late one night when a fellow-guest approached him.

"Saw you did n't remember me at dinner."

The voice was hesitating, pleasant, and not quite unfamiliar. The consul looked up, and identified the figure before him as one of the new arrivals that day, whom, in the informal and easy courtesy of the house, he had met with no further introduction than a vague smile. He remembered, too, that the stranger had glanced at him once or twice at dinner, with shy but engaging reserve.

"You must see such a lot of people, and the way things are arranged and settled here everybody expects to look and act like everybody else, don't you know, so you can't tell one chap from another. Deuced annoying, eh? That 's where you Americans are different, and that 's why those countrywomen of yours were so charming, don't you know, so original. We were all together on the top of a coach in Scotland, don't you remember? Had such a jolly time in the beastly rain. You did n't catch my name. It 's Duncaster."

The consul at once recalled his former fellow-traveler. The two men shook hands. The Englishman took a pipe from his smoking-jacket, and drew a chair beside the consul.

"Yes," he continued, comfortably filling his pipe, "the daughter, Miss Kirkby, was awfully good fun; so fresh, so perfectly natural and innocent, don't you know, and yet so extraordinarily sharp and clever. She had some awfully good chaff over that Scotch scenery before those Scotch tourists, do you remember? And it was all so beastly true, too. Perhaps she 's with you here?"

There was so much unexpected and unaffected interest in the young Englishman's eyes that the consul was quite serious in his regrets that the ladies had gone back to Paris.

"I 'd like to have taken them over to Audrey Edge from here. It 's no distance by train. I did ask them in Scotland, but I suppose they had something better to do.

But you might tell them I 've got some sisters there, and that it is an old place and not half bad, don't you know, when you write to them. You might give me their address."

The consul did so, and added a few pleasant words regarding their position, — barring the syndicate, — which he had gathered from Custer. Lord Duncaster's look of interest, far from abating, became gently confidential.

"I suppose you must see a good deal of your countrymen in your business, and I suppose, just like Englishmen, they differ, by Jove! Some of them, don't you know, are rather pushing and anxious for position, and all that sort of thing; and some of 'em, like your friends, are quite independent and natural."

He stopped, and puffed slowly at his pipe. Presently he took it from his mouth, with a little laugh. "I 've a mind to tell you a rather queer experience of mine. It 's nothing against your people generally, you know, nor do I fancy it 's even an American type; so you won't mind my speaking of it. I 've got some property in Scotland, — rather poor stuff you 'd call it, — but, by Jove! some Americans have been laying claim to it under some obscure plea of relationship. There might have been something in it, although not all they claim, but my business man, a clever chap up in your place, — perhaps you may have heard of him, Sir James MacFen, — wrote to me that what they really wanted were some ancestral lands with the right to use the family name and privileges. The oddest part of the affair was that the claimant was an impossible sort of lunatic, and the whole thing was run by a syndicate of shrewd Western men. As I don't care for the property, which has only been dropping a lot of money every year for upkeep and litigation, Sir James, who is an awfully far-sighted chap at managing, thought he could effect a compromise, and get rid of the property at a fair valuation. And, by Jove! he did. But what your countrymen can get out of it, — for the shooting is n't half as good as what they can get in their own country, — or what use the privileges are to them, I can't fancy."

"I think I know the story," said the consul, eying his fellow-guest attentively; "but if I remember rightly, the young man claimed to be the rightful and only surviving heir."

The Englishman rose, and, bending over the hearth, slowly knocked the ashes from his pipe. "That's quite impossible, don't you know. For," he added, as he stood up in front of the fire in face, figure, and careless repose more decidedly English than ever, "you see my title of Duncaster only came to me through an uncle, but I am the direct and sole heir of the old family, and the Scotch property. I don't perhaps look like a Scot, — we've been settled in England some time, — but," he continued with an invincible English drawling deliberation, " *I*—am—really—you—know—what they call The McHulish."

AN EPISODE OF WEST WOODLANDS.

I.

THE rain was dripping monotonously from the scant eaves of the little church of the Sidon Brethren at West Woodlands. Hewn out of the very heart of a thicket of buckeye spruce and alder, unsunned and unblown upon by any wind, it was so green and unseasoned in its solitude that it seemed a part of the arboreal growth, and on damp Sundays to have taken root again and sprouted. There were moss and shining spots on the underside of the unplaned rafters, little green pools of infusoria stood on the ledge of the windows whose panes were at times suddenly clouded by mysterious unknown breaths from without or within. It was oppressed with an extravagance of leaves at all seasons, whether in summer, when green and limp they crowded the porch, doorways, and shutters, or when penetrating knot-holes and interstices of shingle and clapboard, on some creeping vine, they unexpectedly burst and bourgeoned on the walls like banners; or later, when they rotted in brown heaps in corners, outlined the edges of the floor with a thin yellow border, or invaded the ranks of the high-backed benches which served as pews.

There had been a continuous rustling at the porch and the shaking out of waterproofs and closing of umbrellas until the half-filled church was already redolent of damp dyes and the sulphur of India rubber. The eyes of the congregation were turned to the door with something more than the usual curiosity and expectation. For the new revivalist preacher from Horse Shoe Bay was coming that morning. Already voices of authority were heard approaching, and keeping up their conversation to the very door of the sacred edifice in marked contrast with the awed and bashful whisperings in the porch of the ordinary congregation. The worshipers recognized the voices of Deacons Shadwell and Bradley; in the reverential hush of the building they seemed charged with undue importance.

"It was set back in the road for quiet in the Lord's work," said Bradley.

"Yes, but it oughtn't be hidden! Let

your light so shine before men, you know, Brother Bradley," returned a deep voice, unrecognized and unfamiliar — presumably that of the newcomer.

"It would n't take much to move it — on skids and rollers — nearer to the road," suggested Shadwell tentatively.

"No, but if you left it stranded there in the wind and sun, green and sappy as it is now, ye 'd have every seam and crack start-in' till the ribs shone through, and no amount of calkin' would make it water-tight agin. No; my idea is — clear out the brush and shadder around it! Let the light shine in upon it! Make the waste places glad around it, but keep it *there!* And that 's my idea o' gen'ral missionary work; that 's how the gospel orter be rooted."

Here the bell, which from the plain open four-posted belfry above had been clanging with a metallic sharpness that had an odd impatient worldliness about it, suddenly ceased.

"That bell," said Bradley's voice, with the same suggestion of conveying important truths to the listening congregation within, "was took from the wreck of the Tamalpais.

Brother Horley bought it at auction at Horse Shoe Bay and presented it. You know the Tamalpais ran ashore on Skinner's Reef, jest off here."   .

"Yes, with plenty of sea room, not half a gale o' wind blowing, and her real course fifty miles to westward! The whole watch must have drunk or sunk in slothful idleness," returned the deep voice again. A momentary pause followed, and then the two deacons entered the church with the stranger.

He appeared to be a powerfully-built man, with a square, beardless chin; a face that carried one or two scars of smallpox and a deeper one of a less peaceful suggestion, set in a complexion weather-beaten to the color of Spanish leather. Two small, moist gray eyes, that glistened with every emotion, seemed to contradict the hard expression of the other features. He was dressed in cheap black, like the two deacons, with the exception of a loose, black alpaca coat and the usual black silk neckerchief tied in a large bow under a turndown collar, — the general sign and symbol of a minister of his sect. He walked directly to the raised platform at the end of the chapel, where stood a table on which was a pitcher of water, a glass and hymn-book, and a tall upright desk holding a Bible. Glancing over these details, he suddenly paused, carefully lifted some hitherto undetected object from the desk beside the Bible, and, stooping gently, placed it upon the floor. As it hopped away the congregation saw that it was a small green frog. The intrusion was by no means an unusual one, but some odd contrast between this powerful man and the little animal affected them profoundly. No one — even the youngest — smiled; every one — even the youngest — became suddenly attentive. Turning over the leaves of the hymn-book, he then gave out the first two lines of a hymn. The choir accordion in the front side bench awoke like an infant into wailing life, and Cissy Appleby, soprano, took up a little more musically the lugubrious chant. At the close of the verse the preacher joined in, after a sailor fashion, with a breezy bass that seemed to fill the little building with the trouble of the sea. Then followed prayer from Deacon Shadwell, broken by "Amens" from the preacher, with a nautical suggestion of

"Ay, ay," about them, and he began his sermon.

It was, as those who knew his methods might have expected, a suggestion of the conversation they had already overheard. He likened the little chapel, choked with umbrage and rotting in its dampness, to the gospel seed sown in crowded places, famishing in the midst of plenty, and sterile from the absorptions of the more active life around it. He pointed out again the true work of the pioneer missionary; the careful pruning and elimination of those forces that grew up with the Christian's life, which many people foolishly believed were a part of it. "The *World* must live and the *Word* must live," said they, and there were easy-going brethren who thought they could live together. But he warned them that the World was always closing upon — "shaddering " — and strangling the Word, unless kept down, and that "fair seemin' settlement," or city, which appeared to be "bustin' and bloomin'" with life and progress, was really "hustlin' and jostlin'" the Word of God, even in the midst of these "fancy spires and steeples" it had erected to its glory. It was the work of the missionary pioneer to keep down or root out this carnal, worldly growth as much in. the settlement as in the wilderness. Some were for getting over the difficulty by dragging the mere wasted "letter of the Word," or the rotten and withered husks of it, into the highways and byways, where the "blazin'" scorn of the World would finish it. A low, penitential groan from Deacon Shadwell followed this accusing illustration. But the preacher would tell them that the only way was to boldly attack this rankly growing World around them; to clear out fresh paths for the Truth, and let the sunlight of Heaven stream among them.

There was little doubt that the congregation was moved. Whatever they might have thought of the application, the fact itself was patent. The rheumatic Beaseleys felt the truth of it in their aching bones; it came home to the fever and ague stricken Filgees in their damp seats against the sappy wall; it echoed plainly in the chronic cough of Sister Mary Strutt and Widow Doddridge; and Cissy Appleby, with her round brown eyes fixed upon the speaker, remembering how the starch had been taken out of her Sunday frocks, how her long ringlets had become uncurled, her frills limp, and even her ribbons lustreless, felt that indeed a prophet had arisen in Israel!

One or two, however, were disappointed that he had as yet given no indication of that powerful exhortatory emotion for which he was famed, and which had been said to excite certain corresponding corybantic symptoms among his sensitive female worshipers. When the service was over, and the congregation crowded around him, Sister Mary Strutt, on the outer fringe of the assembly, confided to Sister Evans that she had "hearn tell how that when he was over at Soquel he prayed that pow'ful that all the wimmen got fits and tremblin' spells, and ole Mrs. Jackson had to be hauled off his legs that she was kneelin' and claspin' while wrestling with the Sperit."

"I reckon we seemed kinder strange to him this morning, and he wanted to jest feel his way to our hearts first," exclaimed Brother Jonas Steers politely. "He 'll be more at home at evenin' service. It 's queer that some of the best exhortin' work is done arter early candlelight. I reckon he 's goin' to stop over with Deacon Bradley to dinner."

But it appeared that the new preacher, now formally introduced as Brother Seabright, was intending to walk over to Hemlock Mills to dinner. He only asked to be directed the nearest way; he would not trouble Brother Shadwell or Deacon Bradley to come with him.

"But here's Cissy Appleby lives within a mile o' thar, and you could go along with her. She'd jest admire to show you the way," interrupted Brother Shadwell. "Wouldn't you, Cissy?"

Thus appealed to, the young chorister — a tall girl of sixteen or seventeen — timidly raised her eyes to Brother Seabright as he was about to repeat his former protestation, and he stopped.

"Ef the young lady *is* goin' that way, it's only fair to accept her kindness in a Christian sperit," he said gently.

Cissy turned with a mingling of apology and bashfulness towards a young fellow who seemed to be acting as her escort, but who was hesitating in an equal bashfulness, when Seabright added: "And perhaps our young friend will come too?"

But the young friend drew back with a confused laugh, and Brother Seabright and

Cissy passed out from the porch together. For a few moments they mingled with the stream and conversation of the departing congregation, but presently Cissy timidly indicated a diverging bypath, and they both turned into it.

It was much warmer in the open than it had been in the chapel and thicket, and Cissy, by way of relieving a certain awkward tension of silence, took off the waterproof cloak and slung it on her arm. This disclosed her five long brown cable-like curls that hung down her shoulders, reaching below her waist in some forgotten fashion of girlhood. They were Cissy's peculiar adornment, remarkable for their length, thickness, and the extraordinary youthfulness imparted to a figure otherwise precociously matured. In some wavering doubt of her actual years and privileges, Brother Seabright offered to carry her cloak for her, but she declined it with a rustic and youthful pertinacity that seemed to settle the question. In fact, Cissy was as much embarrassed as she was flattered by the company of this distinguished stranger. However, it would be known to all West Woodland that he had walked home with her, while nobody but herself would know that they had scarcely exchanged a word. She noticed how he lounged on with a heavy, rolling gait, sometimes a little before or behind her as the path narrowed. At such times when they accidentally came in contact in passing, she felt a half uneasy, physical consciousness of him, which she referred to his size, the scars on his face, or some latent hardness of expression, but was relieved to see that he had not observed it. Yet this was the man that made grown women cry; she thought of old Mrs. Jackson fervently grasping the plodding ankles before her, and a hysteric desire to laugh, with the fear that he might see it on her face, overcame her. Then she wondered if he was going to walk all the way home without speaking, yet she knew she would be more embarrassed if he began to talk to her.

Suddenly he stopped, and she bumped up against him.

"Oh, excuse me!" she stammered hurriedly.

"Eh?" He evidently had not noticed the collision. "Did you speak?"

"No!—that is—it wasn't anything," returned the girl, coloring.

But he had quite forgotten her, and was looking intently before him. They had come to a break in the fringe of woodland, and upon a sudden view of the ocean. At this point the low line of coast-range which sheltered the valley of West Woodlands was abruptly cloven by a gorge that crumbled and fell away seaward to the shore of Horse Shoe Bay. On its northern trend stretched the settlement of Horse Shoe to the promontory of Whale Mouth Point, with its outlying reef of rocks curved inwards like the vast submerged jaw of some marine monster, through whose blunt, tooth-like projections the ship-long swell of the Pacific streamed and fell. On the southern shore the light yellow sands of Punta de las Concepcion glittered like sunshine all the way to the olive-gardens and white domes of the Mission. The two shores seemed to typify the two different climates and civilizations separated by the bay.

The heavy, woodland atmosphere was quickened by the salt breath of the sea. The stranger inhaled it meditatively.

"That's the reef where the Tamalpais struck," he said, "and more 'n fifty miles out of her course — yes, more 'n fifty miles from where she should have bin! It don't look nat'ral. No — it — don't — look — nat'ral!"

As he seemed to be speaking to himself, the young girl, who had been gazing with far greater interest at the foreign-looking southern shore, felt confused and did not reply. Then, as if recalling her presence, Brother Seabright turned to her and said: —

"Yes, young lady; and when you hear the old bell of the Tamalpais, and think of how it came here, you may rejoice in the goodness of the Lord that made even those who strayed from the straight course and the true reckoning the means of testifying onto Him."

But the young are quicker to detect attitudes and affectation than we are apt to imagine; and Cissy could distinguish a certain other straying in this afterthought or moral of the preacher called up by her presence, and knew that it was not the real interest which the view had evoked. She had heard that he had been a sailor, and, with the tact of her sex, answered with what she thought would entertain him: —

"I was a little girl when it happened,

and I heard that some sailors got ashore down there, and climbed up this gully from the rocks below. And they camped that night — for there were no houses at West Woodlands then — just in the woods where our chapel now stands. It was funny, was n't it? — I mean," she corrected herself bashfully, "it was strange they chanced to come just there?"

But she had evidently hit the point of interest.

"What became of them?" he said quickly. "They never came to Horse Shoe Settlement, where the others landed from the wreck. I never heard of that boat's crew or of *any* landing *here*."

"No. They kept on over the range south to the Mission. I reckon they did n't know there was a way down on this side to Horse Shoe," returned Cissy.

Brother Seabright moved on and continued his slow, plodding march. But he kept a little nearer Cissy, and she was conscious that he occasionally looked at her. Presently he said: —

"You have a heavenly gift, Miss Appleby."

Cissy flushed, and her hand involuntarily

went to one of her long, distinguishing
curls. It might be *that*. The preacher
continued : —

"Yes; a voice like yours is a heavenly
gift. And you have properly devoted it to
His service. Have you been singing long?"

"About two years. But I 've got to
study a heap yet."

"The little birds don't think it necessary
to study to praise Him," said the preacher
sententiously.

It occurred to Cissy that this was very
unfair argument. She said quickly : —

"But the little birds don't have to follow words in the hymn-books. You don't
give out lines to larks and bobolinks," and
blushed.

The preacher smiled. It was a very
engaging smile, Cissy thought, that lightened his hard mouth. It enabled her to
take heart of grace, and presently to chatter
like the very birds she had disparaged.
Oh yes; she knew she had to learn a great
deal more. She had studied "some" already. She was taking lessons over at
Point Concepcion, where her aunt had
friends, and she went three times a week.
The gentleman who taught her was not a

Catholic, and, of course, he knew she was a Protestant. She would have preferred to live there, but her mother and father were both dead, and had left her with her aunt. She liked it better because it was sunnier and brighter there. She loved the sun and warmth. She had listened to what he had said about the dampness and gloom of the chapel. It was true. The dampness was that dreadful sometimes it just ruined her clothes, and even made her hoarse. Did he think they would really take his advice and clear out the woods round the chapel?

"Would you like it?" he asked pleasantly.

"Yes."

"And you think you would n't pine so much for the sunshine and warmth of the Mission?"

"I 'm not pining," said Cissy with a toss of her curls, "for anything or anybody; but I think the woods ought to be cleared out. It 's just as it was when the runaways hid there."

"When the *runaways hid there!*" said Brother Seabright quickly. "What runaways?"

"Why, the boat's crew," said Cissy.

"Why do you call them runaways?"

"I don't know. Did n't *you?*" said Cissy simply. "Did n't you say they never came back to Horse Shoe Bay. Perhaps I had it from aunty. But I know it 's damp and creepy; and when I was littler I used to be frightened to be alone there practicing."

"Why?" said the preacher quickly.

"Oh, I don't know," hurried on Cissy, with a vague impression that she had said too much. "Only my fancy, I guess."

"Well," said Brother Seabright after a pause ; "we 'll see what can be done to make a clearing there. Birds sing best in the sunshine, and *you* ought to have some say about it."

Cissy's dimples and blushes came together this time. "That 's our house," she said suddenly, with a slight accent of relief, pointing to a weather-beaten farmhouse on the edge of the gorge. "I turn off here, but you keep straight on for the Mills; they 're back in the woods a piece. But," she stammered with a sudden sense of shame of forgotten hospitality, "won't you come in and see aunty?"

"No, thank you, not now." He stopped,

turning his gaze from the house to her. "How old is your house?   Was it there at the time of the wreck?"

"Yes," said Cissy.

"It 's odd that the crew did not come there for help, eh?"

"Maybe they overlooked it in the darkness and the storm," said Cissy simply. "Good-by, sir."

The preacher held her hand for an instant in his powerful, but gently graduated grasp. "Good-by until evening service."

"Yes, sir," said Cissy.

The young girl tripped on towards her house a little agitated and conscious, and yet a little proud as she saw the faces of her aunt, her uncle, her two cousins, and even her discarded escort, Jo Adams, at the windows, watching her.

"So," said her aunt, as she entered breathlessly, " ye walked home with the preacher!   It was a speshal providence and manifestation for ye, Cissy.   I hope ye was mannerly and humble — and profited by the words of grace."

"I don't know," said Cissy, putting aside her hat and cloak listlessly.   "He did n't talk much of anything — but the old wreck of the Tamalpais."

"What?" said her aunt quickly.

"The wreck of the Tamalpais, and the boat's crew that came up the gorge," repeated the young girl.

"And what did *he* know about the boat's crew?" said her aunt hurriedly, fixing her black eyes on Cissy.

"Nothing except what I told him."

"What *you* told him!" echoed her aunt, with an ominous color filling the sallow hollows of her cheek.

"Yes! He has been a sailor, you know — and I thought it would interest him; and it did! He thought it strange."

"Cecilia Jane Appleby," said her aunt shrilly, "do you mean to say that you threw away your chances of salvation and saving grace just to tell gossiping tales that you knew was lies, and evil report, and false witnesses!"

"I only talked of what I'd heard, aunt Vashti," said Cecilia indignantly. "And he afterwards talked of — of — my voice, and said I had a heavenly gift," she added, with a slight quiver of her lip.

Aunt Vashti regarded the girl sharply.

"And you may thank the Lord for that heavenly gift," she said, in a slightly lowered voice; "for ef ye had n't to use it to-night, I 'd shut ye up in your room, to make it pay for yer foolish gaddin' *tongue!* And I reckon I 'll escort ye to chapel to-night myself, miss, and get shut o' some of this foolishness."

II.

The broad plaza of the Mission de la Concepcion had been baking in the day-long sunlight. Shining drifts from the outlying sand dunes, blown across the ill-paved roadway, radiated the heat in the faces of the few loungers like the pricking of liliputian arrows, and invaded even the cactus hedges. The hot air visibly quivered over the dark red tiles of the tienda roof as if they were undergoing a second burning. The black shadow of a chimney on the whitewashed adobe wall was like a door or cavernous opening in the wall itself; the tops of the olive and pear trees seen above it were russet and sere already in the fierce light. Even the moist breath of the sea beyond had quite evaporated before it crossed the plaza, and now rustled the leaves in the Mission garden with a dry, crepitant sound.

Nevertheless, it seemed to Cissy Appleby, as she crossed the plaza, a very welcome change from West Woodlands. Although the late winter rains had ceased a month ago, — a few days after the revivalist preacher had left, — the woods around the chapel were still sodden and heavy, and the threatened improvement in its site had not taken place. Neither had the preacher himself alluded to it again; his evening sermon — the only other one he preached there — was unexciting, and he had, in fact, left West Woodlands without any display of that extraordinary exhortatory faculty for which he was famous. Yet Cissy, in spite of her enjoyment of the dry, hot Mission, remembered him, and also recalled, albeit poutingly, his blunt suggesting that she was "pining for it." Nevertheless, she would like to have sung for him *here* — supposing it was possible to conceive of a Sidon Brotherhood Chapel at the Mission. It was a great pity, she thought, that the Sidon Brotherhood and the Franciscan Brotherhood were not more brotherly *towards each other*. Cissy belonged to the former by hereditary right, locality, and circumstance, but it is to be feared that her theology was imperfect.

She entered a lane between the Mission wall and a lighter iron fenced inclosure, once a part of the garden, but now the appurtenance of a private dwelling that was reconstructed over the heavy adobe shell of some forgotten structure of the old ecclesiastical founders. It was pierced by many windows and openings, and that sunlight and publicity which the former padres had jealously excluded was now wooed from long balconies and verandas by the new proprietor, a well to do American. Elisha Braggs, whose name was generously and euphoniously translated by his native neighbors into "Don Eliseo," although a heretic, had given largess to the church in the way of restoring its earthquake-shaken tower, and in presenting a new organ to its dilapidated choir. He had further endeared himself to the conservative Spanish population by introducing no obtrusive improvements; by distributing his means through the old channels; by apparently inciting no further alien immigration, but contenting himself to live alone among them, adopting their habits, customs, and language. A harmless musical taste, and a disposition to instruct the young boy choristers, was equally balanced by great skill in horsemanship and the personal management of a ranche of wild cattle on the inland plains.

Consciously pretty, and prettily conscious in her white-starched, rose-sprigged muslin, her pink parasol, beribboned gypsy hat, and the long mane-like curls that swung over her shoulders, Cissy entered the house and was shown to the large low drawing-room on the ground-floor. She once more inhaled its hot potpourri fragrance, in which the spice of the Castilian rose-leaves of the garden was dominant. A few boys, whom she recognized as the choristers of the Mission and her fellow - pupils, were already awaiting her with some degree of anxiety and impatience. This fact, and a certain quick animation that sprang to the blue eyes of the master of the house as the rose-sprigged frock and long curls appeared at the doorway, showed that Cissy was clearly the favorite pupil.

Elisha Braggs was a man of middle age, with a figure somewhat rounded by the adipose curves of a comfortable life, and an air of fastidiousness which was, however, occasionally at variance with what seemed to be his original condition. He greeted

Cissy with a certain nervous overconscious-
ness of his duties as host and teacher, and
then plunged abruptly into the lesson. It
lasted an hour, Cissy tactfully dividing his
somewhat exclusive instruction with the
others, and even interpreting it to their
slower comprehension. When it was over,
the choristers shyly departed, according
to their usual custom, leaving Cissy and
Don Eliseo — and occasionally one of the
padres — to more informal practicing and
performance. Neither the ingenuousness
of Cissy nor the worldly caution of aunt
Vashti had ever questioned the propriety of
these prolonged and secluded *séances;* and
the young girl herself, although by no means
unaccustomed to the bashful attentions of
the youth of West Woodlands, had never
dreamed of these later musical interviews
as being anything but an ordinary recreation of her art. The feeling of gratitude
and kindness she had for Don Eliseo, her
aunt's friend, had never left her conscious
or embarrassed when she was alone with
him. But to-day, possibly from his own
nervousness and preoccupation, she was
aware of some vague uneasiness, and at an
early opportunity rose to go. But Don

Eliseo gently laid his hand on hers and said : —

"Don't go yet; I want to talk to you."

His touch suddenly reminded her that once or twice before he had done the same thing, and she had been disagreeably impressed by it. But she lifted her brown eyes to his with an unconsciousness that was more crushing than a withdrawal of her hand, and waited for him to go on.

"It is such a long way for you to come, and you have so little time to stay when you are here, that I am thinking of asking your aunt to let you live here at the Mission, as a pupil, in the house of the Señora Hernandez, until your lessons are finished. Padre José will attend to the rest of your education. Would you like it?"

Poor Cissy's eyes leaped up in unaffected and sparkling affirmation before her tongue replied. To bask in this beloved sunshine for days together; to have this quaint Spanish life before her eyes, and those soft Spanish accents in her ears; to forget herself in wandering in the old-time Mission garden beyond; to have daily access to Mr. Braggs's piano and the organ of the church — this was indeed the realization of her fondest dreams! Yet she hesitated. Somewhere in her inherited Puritan nature was a vague conviction that it was wrong, and it seemed even to find an echo in the warning of the preacher: this was what she was "pining for."

"I don't know," she stammered. "I must ask auntie; I should n't like to leave her; and there 's the chapel."

"Is n't that revivalist preacher enough to run it for a while?" said her companion, half-sneeringly.

The remark was not a tactful one.

"Mr. Seabright has n't been here for a month," she answered somewhat quickly. "But he 's coming next Sunday, and I 'm glad of it. He 's a very good man. And there 's nothing he don't notice. He saw how silly it was to stick the chapel into the very heart of the woods, and he told them so."

"And I suppose he 'll run up a brand-new meeting-house out on the road," said Braggs, smiling.

"No, he 's going to open up the woods, and let the sun and light in, and clear out the underbrush."

"And what 's that for?"

There was such an utter and abrupt change in the speaker's voice and manner — which until then had been lazily fastidious and confident — that Cissy was startled. And the change being rude and dictatorial, she was startled into opposition. She had wanted to say that the improvement had been suggested by *her*, but she took a more aggressive attitude.

"Brother Seabright says it's a question of religion and morals. It's a scandal and a wrong, and a disgrace to the Word, that the chapel should have been put there."

Don Eliseo's face turned so white and waxy that Cissy would have noticed it had she not femininely looked away while taking this attitude.

"I suppose that's a part of his sensation style, and very effective," he said, resuming his former voice and manner. "I must try to hear him some day. But, now, in regard to your coming here, of course I shall consult your aunt, although I imagine she will have no objection. I only wanted to know how *you* felt about it." He again laid his hand on hers.

"I should like to come very much," said Cissy timidly; "and it's very kind of you,

I 'm sure; but you 'll see what auntie says, won't you?" She withdrew her hand after momentarily grasping his, as if his own act had been only a parting salutation, and departed.

Aunt Vashti received Cissy's account of her interview with a grim satisfaction. She did not know what ideas young gals had nowadays, but in *her* time she 'd been fit to jump outer her skin at such an offer from such a good man as Elisha Braggs. And he was a rich man, too. And ef he was goin' to give her an edication free, it was n't goin' to stop there. For her part, she did n't like to put ideas in young girls' heads, — goodness knows they 'd enough foolishness already; but if Cissy made a Christian use of her gifts, and 'tended to her edication and privileges, and made herself a fit helpmeet for any man, she would say that there were few men in these parts that was as " comf'ble ketch " as Lish Braggs, or would make as good a husband and provider.

The blood suddenly left Cissy's cheeks and then returned with uncomfortable heat. Her annt's words had suddenly revealed to her the meaning of the uneasiness she had felt in Braggs's house that morning — the old repulsion that had come at his touch. She had never thought of him as a suitor or a beau before, yet it now seemed perfectly plain to her that this was the ulterior meaning of his generosity. And yet she received that intelligence with the same mixed emotions with which she had received his offer to educate her. She did not conceal from herself the pride and satisfaction she felt in this presumptive selection of her as his wife; the worldly advantages that it promised; nor that it was a destiny far beyond her deserts. Yet she was conscious of exactly the same sense of wrong-doing in her preferences — something that seemed vaguely akin to that "conviction of sin" of which she had heard so much — as when she received his offer of education. It was this mixture of fear and satisfaction that caused her alternate paling and flushing, yet this time it was the fear that came first. Perhaps she was becoming unduly sensitive. The secretiveness of her sex came to her aid here, and she awkwardly changed the subject. Aunt Vashti, complacently believing that her words had fallen on fruitful soil, discreetly said no more.

It was a hot morning when Cissy walked alone to chapel early next Sunday. There was a dry irritation in the air which even the northwest trades, blowing through the seaward gorge, could not temper, and for the first time in her life she looked forward to the leafy seclusion of the buried chapel with a feeling of longing. She had avoided her youthful escort, for she wished to practice alone for an hour before the service with the new harmonium that had taken the place of the old accordion and its unskillful performer. Perhaps, too, there was a timid desire to be at her best on the return of Brother Seabright, and to show him, with a new performance, that the "heavenly gift" had not been neglected. She opened the chapel with the key she always carried, "swished" away an intrusive squirrel, left the door and window open for a moment, until the beating of frightened wings against the rafters had ceased, and, after carefully examining the floor for spiders, mice, and other creeping things, brushed away a few fallen leaves and twigs from the top of the harmonium. Then, with her long curls tossed over her shoulders and hanging limply down the back of her new maple-leaf yellow frock, — which was also a timid recognition of Brother Seabright's return, — and her brown eyes turned to the rafters, this rustic St. Cecilia of the Coast Range began to sing. The shell of the little building dilated with the melody; the sashes of the windows pulsated, the two ejected linnets joined in timidly from their coign of vantage in the belfry outside, and the limp vines above the porch swayed like her curls. Once she thought she heard stealthy footsteps without; once she was almost certain she felt the brushing of somebody outside against the thin walls of the chapel, and once she stopped to glance quickly at the window with a strange instinct that some one was looking at her. But she quickly reflected that Brother Seabright would come there only when the deacons did, and with them. Why she should think that it was Brother Seabright, or why Brother Seabright should come thus and at such a time, she could not have explained.

He did not, in fact, make his appearance until later, and after the congregation had quite filled the chapel; he did not, moreover, appear to notice her as she sat there, and when he gave out the hymn he seemed to have quietly overlooked the new harmonium. She sang her best, however, and more than one of the audience thought that "little Sister Appleby" had greatly improved. Indeed, it would not have seemed strange to some — remembering Brother Seabright's discursive oratory — if he had made some allusion to it. But he did not. His heavy eyes moved slowly over the congregation, and he began.

As usual he did not take a text. But he would talk to them that morning about "The Conviction of Sin" and the sense of wrong-doing that was innate in the sinner. This included all form of temptation, for what was temptation but the inborn consciousness of something to struggle against, and that was sin! At this apparently concise exposition of her own feelings in regard to Don Eliseo's offer, Cissy felt herself blushing to the roots of her curls. Could it be possible that Brother Seabright had heard of her temptation to leave West Woodlands, and that this warning was intended for her? He did not even look in her direction. Yet his next sentence seemed to be an answer to her own mental query.

"Folks might ask," he continued, "if even the young and inexperienced should feel this — or was there a state of innocent guilt without consciousness?" He would answer that question by telling them what had happened to him that morning. He had come to the chapel, not by the road, but through the tangled woods behind them (Cissy started) — through the thick brush and undergrowth that was choking the life out of this little chapel — the wilderness that he had believed was never before trodden by human feet, and was known only to roaming beasts and vermin. But that was where he was wrong.

In the stillness and listening silence, a sudden cough from some one in one of the back benches produced that instantaneous diversion of attention common to humanity on such occasions. Cissy's curls swung round with the others. But she was surprised to see that Mr. Braggs was seated in one of the benches near the door, and from the fact of his holding a handkerchief to his mouth, and being gazed at by his neighbors, it was evident that it was he who had coughed. Perhaps he had come to West Woodlands to talk to her aunt! With the preacher before her, and her probable suitor behind her, she felt herself again blushing.

Brother Seabright continued. Yes, he was *wrong*, for there before him, in the depths of the forest, were two children. They were looking at a bush of "pizon berries," — the deadly nightshade, as it was fitly called, — and one was warning the other of its dangerous qualities.

"But how do you know it 's the 'pizon berry' ?" asked the other.

"Because it 's larger, and nicer, and bigger, and easier to get than the real good ones," returned the other.

And it was so. Thus was the truth revealed from the mouths of babes and sucklings; even they were conscious of temptation and sin! But here there was another interruption from the back benches, which proved, however, to be only the suppressed giggle of a boy — evidently the youthful hero of the illustration, surprised into nervous hilarity.

The preacher then passed to the "Conviction of Sin" in its more familiar phases. Many brothers confounded this with *discovery* and *publicity*. It was not their own sin "finding them out," but others discovering it. Until that happened, they fancied themselves safe, stilling their consciences, confounding the blinded eye of the world with the all-seeing eye of the Lord. But were they safe even then? Did not sooner or later the sea deliver up its dead, the earth what was buried in it, the wild woods what its depths had hidden? Was not the foolish secret, the guilty secret, the forgotten sin, sure to be disclosed? Then if they could not fly from the testimony of His works, if they could not evade even their fellow-man, why did they not first turn to Him? Why, from the penitent child at his mother's knee to the murderer on the scaffold, did they only at *the last* confess unto Him?

His voice and manner had suddenly changed. From the rough note of accusation and challenge it had passed into the equally rough, but broken and sympathetic, accents of appeal. Why did they hesitate longer to confess their sin — not to man — but unto Him? Why did they delay? Now — that evening! That very moment! This was the appointed time! He entreated them in the name of religious faith, in the name of a human brotherly love. His delivery was now no longer deliberate, but hurried and panting; his speech now no longer chosen, but made up of reiterations and repetitions, ejaculations, and even incoherent epithets. His gestures and long intonations which began to take the place of even that interrupted speech affected them more than his reasoning! Short sighs escaped them; they swayed to and fro with the rhythm of his voice and movements. They had begun to comprehend this exacerbation of emotion — this paroxysmal rhapsody. This was the dithyrambic exaltation they had ardently waited for. They responded quickly. First with groans, equally inarticulate murmurs of assent, shouts of "Glory," and the reckless invocation of sacred names. Then a wave of hysteria seemed to move the whole mass, and broke into tears and sobs among the women. In her own excited consciousness it seemed to Cissy that some actual struggle between good and evil — like unto the casting out of devils — was shaking the little building. She cast a hurried glance behind her and saw Mr. Braggs sitting erect, white and scornful. She knew that she too was shrinking from the speaker,

— not from any sense of conviction, but because he was irritating and disturbing her innate sense of fitness and harmony, — and she was pained that Mr. Braggs should see him thus. Meantime the weird, invisible struggle continued, heightened and, it seemed to her, incited by the partisan groans and exultant actions of those around her, until suddenly a wild despairing cry arose above the conflict. A vague fear seized her — the voice was familiar! She turned in time to see the figure of aunt Vashti rise in her seat with a hysterical outburst, and fall convulsively forward upon her knees! She would have rushed to her side, but the frenzied woman was instantly caught by Deacon Shadwell and surrounded by a group of her own sex and became hidden. And when Cissy recovered herself she was astonished to find Brother Seabright — with every trace of his past emotion vanished from his hard-set face — calmly taking up his coherent discourse in his ordinary level tones. The furious struggle of the moment before was over; the chapel and its congregation had fallen back into an exhausted and apathetic silence! Then the preacher gave out the hymn — the words were singularly jubilant among that usually mournful collection in the book before her — and Cissy began it with a tremulous voice. But it gained strength, clearness, and volume as she went on, and she felt thrilled throughout with a new human sympathy she had never known before. The preacher's bass supported her now for the first time not unmusically — and the service was over.

Relieved, she turned quickly to join her aunt, but a hand was laid gently upon her shoulder. It was Brother Seabright, who had just stepped from the platform. The congregation, knowing her to be the niece of the hysteric woman, passed out without disturbing them.

"You have, indeed, improved your gift, Sister Cecilia," he said gravely. "You must have practiced much."

"Yes — that is, no! — only a little," stammered Cissy.

"But, excuse me, I must look after auntie," she added, drawing timidly away.

"Your aunt is better, and has gone on with Sister Shadwell. She is not in need of your help, and really would do better without you just now. I shall see her myself presently."

"But *you* made her sick already," said Cissy, with a sudden, half-nervous audacity. "You even frightened *me*."

"Frightened you?" repeated Seabright, looking at her quickly.

"Yes," said Cissy, meeting his gaze with brown, truthful eyes. "Yes, when you — when you — made those faces. I like to hear you talk, but " — she stopped.

Brother Seabright's rare smile again lightened his face. But it seemed sadder than when she had first seen it.

"Then you have been practicing again at the Mission?" he said quietly; "and you still prefer it?"

"Yes," said Cissy. She wanted to appear as loyal to the Mission in Brother Seabright's presence as she was faithful to West Woodlands in Mr. Braggs's. She had no idea that this was dangerously near to coquetry. So she said a little archly, "I don't see why *you* don't like the Mission. You 're a missionary yourself. The old padres came here to spread the Word. So do you."

"But not in that way," he said curtly. "I 've seen enough of them when I was knocking round the world a seafaring man and a sinner. I knew them — receivers of the ill-gotten gains of adventurers, fools, and scoundrels. I knew them — enriched by the spoils of persecution and oppression; gathering under their walls outlaws and fugitives from justice, and flinging an indulgence here and an absolution there, as they were paid for it. Don't talk to me of *them* — I know them."

They were passing out of the chapel together, and he made an impatient gesture as if dismissing the subject. Accustomed though she was to the sweeping criticism of her Catholic friends by her West Woodlands associates, she was nevertheless hurt by his brusqueness. She dropped a little behind, and they separated at the porch. Notwithstanding her anxiety to see her aunt, she felt she could not now go to Deacon Shadwell's without seeming to follow him — and after he had assured her that her help was not required! She turned aside and made her way slowly towards her home.

There she found that her aunt had not returned, gathering from her uncle that she was recovering from a fit of "high strikes" (hysterics), and would be better alone.

Whether he underrated her complaint, or had a consciousness of his masculine helplessness in such disorders, he evidently made light of it. And when Cissy, afterwards, a little ashamed that she had allowed her momentary pique against Brother Seabright to stand in the way of her duty, determined to go to her aunt, instead of returning to the chapel that evening, he did not oppose it. She learned also that Mr. Braggs had called in the morning, but, finding that her aunt Vashti was at chapel, he had followed her there, intending to return with her. But he had not been seen since the service, and had evidently returned to the Mission.

But when she reached Deacon Shadwell's house she was received by Mrs. Shadwell only. Her aunt, said that lady, was physically better, but Brother Seabright had left "partkler word" that she was to see nobody. It was an extraordinary case of "findin' the Lord," the like of which had never been known before in West Woodlands, and she (Cissy) would yet be proud of one of her "fammerly being speshally selected for grace." But the "workin's o' salvation was not to be finicked away on worldly things or even the affections of the flesh;" and if Cissy really loved her aunt, "she wouldn't interfere with her while she was, so to speak, still on the mourners' bench, wrastlin' with the Sperret in their back sittin'-room." But she might wait until Brother Seabright's return from evening chapel after service.

Cissy waited. Nine o'clock came, but Brother Seabright did not return. Then a small but inconsequent dignity took possession of her, and she slightly tossed her long curls from her shoulders. She was not going to wait for any man's permission to see her own aunt. If auntie did not want to see her, that was enough. She could go home alone. She didn't want any one to go with her.

Lifted and sustained by these loftly considerations, with an erect head and slightly ruffled mane, well enwrapped in a becoming white merino "cloud," the young girl stepped out on her homeward journey. She had certainly enough to occupy her mind and, perhaps, justify her independence. To have a suitor for her hand in the person of the superior and wealthy Mr. Braggs, — for that was what his visit that morning to West Woodlands meant, — and to be personally complimented on her improvement by the famous Brother Seabright, all within twelve hours, was something to be proud of, even although it was mitigated by her aunt's illness, her suitor's abrupt departure, and Brother Seabright's momentary coldness and impatience. Oddly enough, this last and apparently trivial circumstance occupied her thoughts more than the others. She found herself looking out for him in the windings of the moonlit road, and when, at last, she reached the turning towards the little wood and chapel, her small feet unconsciously lingered until she felt herself blushing under her fleecy "cloud." She looked down the lane. From the point where she was standing the lights of the chapel should have been plainly visible; but now all was dark. It was nearly ten o'clock, and he must have gone home by another road. Then a spirit of adventure seized her. She had the key of the chapel in her pocket. She remembered she had left a small black Spanish fan — a former gift of Mr. Braggs — lying on the harmonium. She would go and bring it away, and satisfy herself that

Brother Seabright was not there still. It was but a step, and in the clear moonlight.

The lane wound before her like a silver stream, except where it was interrupted and bridged over by jagged black shadows. The chapel itself was black, the clustering trees around it were black also; the porch seemed to cover an inky well of shadow; the windows were rayless and dead, and in the chancel one still left open showed a yawning vault of obscurity within. Nevertheless, she opened the door softly, glided into the dark depths, and made her way to the harmonium. But here the sound of footsteps without startled her; she glanced hurriedly through the open window, and saw the figure of Elisha Braggs suddenly revealed in the moonlight as he crossed the path behind the chapel. He was closely followed by two peons, whom she recognized as his servants at the Mission, and they each carried a pickaxe. From their manner it was evident that they had no suspicion of her presence in the chapel. But they had stopped and were listening. Her heart beat quickly; with a sudden instinct she ran and bolted the door. But it was evidently another intruder they were watch-

ing, for she presently saw Brother Seabright quietly cross the lane and approach
the chapel. The three men had disappeared; but there was a sudden shout, the
sound of scuffling, the deep voice of Brother
Seabright saying, "Back, there, will you!
Hands off!" and a pause. She could see
nothing; she listened in every pulse. Then
the voice of Brother Seabright arose again
quite clearly, slowly, and as deliberately as
if it had risen from the platform in the
chapel.

"Lish Barker! I thought as much!
Lish Barker, first mate of the Tamalpais,
who was said to have gone down with a
boat's crew and the ship's treasure after she
struck. I *thought* I knew that face to-
day."

"Yes," said the voice of him whom she
had known as Elisha Braggs, — "yes, and
I knew *your* face, Jim Seabright, ex-
whaler, slaver, pirate, and bo's'n of the
Highflyer, marooned in the South Pacific,
where you found the Lord — ha! ha! —
and became the psalm-singing, converted
American sailor preacher!"

"I am not ashamed before men of my
past, which every one knows," returned

Seabright slowly. "But what of *yours*, Elisha Barker — *yours* that has made you sham death itself to hide it from them? What of *yours* — spent in the sloth of your ill-gotten gains! Turn, sinner, turn! Turn, Elisha Braggs, while there is yet time!"

"Belay there, Brother Seabright; we're not *inside* your gospel-shop just now! Keep your palaver for those that need it. Let me pass, before I have to teach you that you have n't to deal with a gang of hysterical old women to-night."

"But not until you know that one of those women, — Vashti White, — by God's grace converted of her sins, has confessed her secret and yours, Elisha Barker! Yes! She has told me how her sister's husband — the father of the young girl you are trying to lure away — helped you off that night with your booty, took his miserable reward and lived and died in exile with the rest of your wretched crew, — afraid to return to his home and country — whilst you — shameless and impenitent — lived in slothful ease at the Mission!"

"Liar! Let me pass!"

"Not until I know your purpose here to-night."

"Then take the consequences! Here, Pedro! Ramon! Seize him. Tie him head and heels together, and toss him in the bush!"

The sound of scuffling recommenced. The struggle seemed fierce and long, with no breath wasted in useless outcry. Then there was a bright flash, a muffled report, and the stinging and fire of gunpowder at the window.

Transfixed with fear, Cissy cast a despairing glance around her. Ah, the bell-rope! In another instant she had grasped it frantically in her hands.

All the fear, indignation, horror, sympathy, and wild appeal for help that had arisen helplessly in her throat and yet remained unuttered, now seemed to thrill through her fingers and the tightened rope, and broke into frantic voice in the clanging metal above her. The whole chapel, the whole woodland, the clear, moonlit sky above was filled with its alarming accents. It shrieked, implored, protested, summoned, and threatened, in one ceaseless outcry, seeming to roll over and over — as, indeed, it did — in leaps and bounds that shook the belfry. Never before, even in the blows of the striking surges, had the bell of the Tamalpais clamored like that! Once she heard above the turmoil the shaking of the door against the bolt that still held firmly; once she thought she heard Seabright's voice calling to her; once she thought she smelled the strong smoke of burning grass. But she kept on, until the window was suddenly darkened by a figure, and Brother Seabright, leaping in, caught her in his arms as she was reeling fainting, but still clinging to the rope. But his strong presence and some powerful magnetism in his touch restored her.

"You have heard all!" he said.

"Yes."

"Then for your aunt's sake, for your dead father's sake, *forget* all! That wretched man has fled with his wounded hirelings — let his sin go with him. But the village is alarmed — the brethren may be here any moment! Neither question nor deny what I shall tell them. Fear nothing. God will forgive the silence that leaves the vengeance to His hands alone!" Voices and footsteps were heard approaching the chapel. Brother Seabright significantly pressed her hand and strode towards the door. Deacon Shadwell was first to enter.

"You here — Brother Seabright! What has happened?"

"God be praised!" said Brother Seabright cheerfully, "nothing of consequence! The danger is over! Yet, but for the courage and presence of mind of Sister Appleby a serious evil might have been done." He paused, and with another voice turned half-interrogatively towards her. "Some children, or a passing tramp, had carelessly thrown matches in the underbrush, and they were ignited beside the chapel. Sister Appleby, chancing to return here for " —

"For my fan," said Cissy with a timid truthfulness of accent.

"Found herself unable to cope with it, and it occurred to her to give the alarm you heard. I happened to be passing and was first to respond. Haply the flames had made but little headway, and were quickly beaten down. It is all over now. But let us hope that the speedy clearing out of the underbrush and the opening of the woods around the chapel will prevent any recurrence of the alarm of to-night."

.   .   .   .

That the lesson thus reiterated by Brother Seabright was effective, the following extract, from the columns of the "Whale Point Gazette," may not only be offered as evidence, but may even give the cautious reader further light on the episode itself: —

STRANGE DISCOVERY AT WEST WOODLANDS. — THE TAMALPAIS MYSTERY AGAIN.

The improvements in the clearing around the Sidon Chapel at West Woodlands, undertaken by the Rev. James Seabright, have disclosed another link in the mystery which surrounded the loss of the Tamalpais some years ago at Whale Mouth Point. It will be remembered that the boat containing Adams & Co.'s treasure, the Tamalpais' first officer, and a crew of four men was lost on the rocks shortly after leaving the ill-fated vessel. None of the bodies were ever recovered, and the treasure itself completely baffled the search of divers and salvers. A lidless box bearing the mark of Adams & Co., of the kind in which their treasure was usually shipped, was yesterday found in the woods behind the chapel, half buried in brush, bark, and windfalls. There were no other indications, except the traces of a camp-fire

at some remote period, probably long before the building of the chapel. But how
and when the box was transported to the
upland, and by whose agency, still remains
a matter of conjecture. Our reporter who
visited the Rev. Mr. Seabright, who has
lately accepted the regular ministry of the
chapel, was offered every facility for in-
formation, but it was evident that the early
settlers who were cognizant of the fact — if
there were any — are either dead or have
left the vicinity.

THE HOME–COMING OF JIM WILKES.

I.

For many minutes there had been no sound but the monotonous drumming of the rain on the roof of the coach, the swishing of wheels through the gravelly mud, and the momentary clatter of hoofs upon some rocky outcrop in the road. Conversation had ceased; the light-hearted young editor in the front seat, more than suspected of dangerous levity, had relapsed into silence since the heavy man in the middle seat had taken to regarding the ceiling with ostentatious resignation, and the thin female beside him had averted her respectable bonnet. An occasional lurch of the coach brought down a fringe of raindrops from its eaves that filmed the windows and shut out the sodden prospect already darkening into night. There had been a momentary relief in their hurried dash through Summit Springs, and the spectacle of certain newly arrived County Delegates crowding the veranda of its one hotel; but that was now three miles behind. The young editor's sole resource was to occasionally steal a glance at the face of the one passenger who seemed to be in sympathy with him, but who was too far away for easy conversation. It was the half-amused, half-perplexed face of a young man who had been for some time regarding him from a remote corner of the coach with an odd mingling of admiring yet cogitating interest, which, however, had never extended to any further encouragement than a faint sad smile. Even this at last faded out in the growing darkness; the powerful coach lamps on either side that flashed on the wayside objects gave no light to the interior. Everybody was slowly falling asleep. Suddenly everybody woke up to find that the coach was apparently standing still! When it had stopped no one knew! The young editor lowered his window. The coach lamp on that side was missing, but nothing was to be seen. In the distance there appeared to be a faint splashing.

"Well," called out an impatient voice from the box above; " what do you make it?" It was the authoritative accents of

Yuba Bill, the driver, and everybody listened eagerly for the reply.

It came faintly from the distance and the splashing. "Almost four feet here, and deepening as you go."

"Dead water?"

"No — back water from the Fork."

There was a general movement towards the doors and windows. The splashing came nearer. Then a light flashed. on the trees, the windows, and — two feet of yellow water peacefully flowing beneath them! The thin female gave a slight scream.

"There 's no danger," said the Expressman, now wading towards them with the coach lamp in his hand. "But we 'll have to' pull round out of it and go back to the Springs. There 's no getting past this break to-night."

"Why did n't you let us know this before," said the heavy man indignantly from the window.

"Jim," said the driver with that slow deliberation which instantly enforced complete attention.

"Yes, Bill."

"Have you got a spare copy of that reg-'lar bulletin that the Stage Kempany issoos every ten minutes to each passenger to tell 'em where we are, how far it is to the next place, and wots the state o' the weather gin'rally?"

"No!" said the Expressman grimly, as he climbed to the box "there's not one left. Why?"

"Cos the Emperor of Chiny's inside wantin' one! Hoop! Keep your seats down there! G'lang!" the whip cracked, there was a desperate splashing, a backward and forward jolting of the coach, the glistening wet flanks and tossing heads of the leaders seen for a moment opposite the windows, a sickening swirl of the whole body of the vehicle as if parting from its axles, a long straight dragging pull, and — presently the welcome sound of hoofs once more beating the firmer ground.

"Hi! Hold up — driver!"

It was the editor's quiet friend who was leaning from the window.

"Isn't Wilkes's ranch just off here?"

"Yes, half a mile along the ridge, I reckon," returned the driver shortly.

"Well, if you're not going on to-night, I'd get off and stop there."

"I reckon your head's level, stranger,"

said Bill approvingly; "for they 're about chock full at the Springs' House."

To descend, the passenger was obliged to pass out by the middle seat and before the young editor. As he did so he cast a shy look on him and, leaning over, said hesitatingly, in a lower voice: "I don't think you will be able to get in at the Springs Hotel. If — if — you care to come with me to — to — the ranch, I can take care of you."

The young editor — a man of action — paused for an instant only. Then seizing his bag, he said promptly: "Thank you," and followed his newly-found friend to the ground. The whip cracked, the coach rolled away.

"You know Wilkes?" he said.

"Ye-ee-s. He 's my father."

"Ah," said the editor cheerfully, "then you 're going home?"

"Yes."

It was quite light in the open, and the stranger, after a moment's survey of the prospect, — a survey that, however, seemed to be characterized by his previous hesitation, — said: "This way," crossed the road, and began to follow a quite plain but long disused wagon track along the slope. His manner was still so embarrassed that the young editor, after gayly repeating his thanks for his companion's thoughtful courtesy, followed him in silence. At the end of ten minutes they had reached some cultivated fields and orchards; the stranger brightened, although still with a preoccupied air, quickened his pace, and then suddenly stopped. When the editor reached his side he was gazing with apparently still greater perplexity upon the level, half obliterated, and blackened foundations of what had been a large farmhouse.

"Why, it's been burnt down!" he said thoughtfully.

The editor stared at him! Burnt down it certainly had been, but by no means recently. Grasses were already springing up from the charred beams in the cellar, vines were trailing over the fallen chimneys, excavations, already old, had been made among the ruins. "When were you here last?" the editor asked abruptly.

"Five years ago," said the stranger abstractedly.

"Five years! — and you knew nothing of *this?*"

"No. I was in Tahiti, Australia, Japan, and China all the time."

"And you never heard from home?"

"No. You see I quo'led with the old man, and ran away."

"And you did n't write to tell them you were coming?"

"No." He hesitated, and then added: "Never thought o' coming till I saw *you.*"

"Me!"

"Yes ; you and — the high water."

"Do you mean to say," said the young editor sharply, " that you brought *me* — an utter stranger to you — out of that coach to claim the hospitality of a father you had quarreled with — had n't seen for five years and did n't know if he would receive you? "

"Yes, — you see that 's just *why* I did it. You see, I reckoned my chances would be better to see him along with a cheerful, chipper fellow like you. I did n't, of course, kalkilate on this," he added, pointing dejectedly to the ruins.

The editor gasped; then a sudden conception of the unrivaled absurdity of the situation flashed upon him, — of his passively following the amiable idiot at his side in order to contemplate, by the falling rain and lonely night, a heap of sodden ruins, while the coach was speeding to Summit Springs and shelter, and, above all, the reason *why* he was invited, — until, putting down his bag, he leaned upon his stick, and laughed until the tears came to his eyes.

At which his companion visibly brightened. "I told you so," he said cheerfully; "I knew you 'd be able to take it — and the old man — in *that way*, and that would have fetched him round."

"For Heaven's sake! don't talk any more," said the editor, wiping his eyes, "but try to remember if you ever had any neighbors about here where we can stay to-night. We can't walk to Summit Springs, and we can't camp out on these ruins."

"There did n't use to be anybody nearer than the Springs."

"But that was five years ago, you say," said the editor impatiently; "and although your father probably moved away after the house burned down, the country 's been thickly settled since then. That field has been lately planted. There must be another house beyond. Let 's follow the trail a little farther."

They tramped along in silence, this time the editor leading. Presently he stopped.

"There's a house — in there — among the trees," he said, pointing. "Whose is it?"

The stranger shook his head dubiously. Although apparently unaffected by any sentimental consideration of his father's misfortune, the spectacle of the blackened ruins of the homestead had evidently shaken his preconceived plans. "It was n't there in *my* time," he said musingly.

"But it *is* there in *our* time," responded the editor briskly, "and *I* propose to go there. From what you have told me of your father — even if his house were still standing — our chances of getting supper and a bed from him would be doubtful! I suppose," he continued as they moved on together, "you left him in anger — five years ago?"

"Ye-es."

"Did he say anything as you left?"

"I don't remember anything particular that he *said*."

"Well, what did he *do?*"

"Shot at me from the window!"

"Ah!" said the young editor softly. Nevertheless they walked on for some time in silence. Gradually a white picket fence came into view at right angles with .the trail, and a man appeared walking leisurely along what seemed to be the regularly traveled road, beside it. The editor, who had taken matters in his own hands, without speaking to his companion, ran quickly forward and accosted the stranger, briefly stating that he had left the stage-coach with a companion, because it was stopped by high water, and asked, without entering into further details, to be directed to some place where they could pass the night. The man quite as briefly directed him to the house among the trees, which he said was his own, and then leisurely pursued his way along the road. The young editor ran back to his companion, who had halted in the dripping shadow of a sycamore, and recounted his good fortune.

"I did n't," he added, "say anything about your father. You can make inquiries yourself later."

" I reckon there won't be much need of that," returned his companion. "You did n't take much note o' that man, did you?"

"Not much," said the editor.

"Well, *that 's my father*, and I reckon that new house must be his."

II.

The young editor was a little startled. The man he had just quitted certainly was not dangerous looking, and yet, remembering what his son had said, there *were* homicidal possibilities. "Look here," he said quickly, "he 's not there *now*. Why don't you seize the opportunity to slip into the house, make peace with your mother and sisters, and get them to intercede with your father when he returns?"

"Thar ain't any mother; she died afore I left. My sister Almiry 's a little girl — though that 's four years ago and mebbee she 's growed. My brothers and me did n't pull together much. But I was thinkin' that mebbee *you* might go in thar for me first, and see how the land lays; then sorter tell 'em 'bout me in your takin', chipper, easy way; make 'em laugh, and when you 've squared 'em — I 'll be hangin' round outside — you kin call *me* in. Don't you see?"

The young editor *did* see. Ridiculous as the proposal would have seemed to him an hour ago, it now appeared practical, and even commended itself to his taste. His name was well known in the county and his mediation might be effective. Perhaps his vanity was slightly flattered by his companion's faith in him; perhaps he was not free from a certain human curiosity to know the rest; perhaps he was more interested than he cared to confess in the helpless home-seeker beside him.

"But you must tell me something more of yourself, and your fortune and prospects. They 'll be sure to ask questions."

"Mebbee they won't. But you can say I 've done well — made my pile over in Australia, and ain't comin' on *them*. Remember — say I ' ain't comin' on them ' ! "

The editor nodded, and then, as if fearful of letting his present impulse cool, ran off towards the house.

It was large and respectable looking, and augured well for the present fortunes of the Wilkes's. The editor had determined to attack the citadel on its weaker, feminine side, and when the front door was opened to his knock, asked to see Miss Almira Wilkes. The Irish servant showed him into a comfortable looking sitting-room, and in another moment with a quick rustle of skirts in the passage a very pretty girl impulsively entered. From the first flash of her keen blue eyes the editor — a fair student of the sex — conceived the idea that she had expected somebody else; from the second that she was an arrant flirt, and did not intend to be disappointed. This much was in his favor.

Spurred by her provoking eyes and the novel situation, he stated his business with an airy lightness and humor that seemed to justify his late companion's estimate of his powers. But even in his cynical attitude he was unprepared for the girl's reception of his news. He had expected some indignation or even harshness towards this man whom he was beginning to consider as a kind of detrimental outcast or prodigal, but he was astounded at the complete and utter indifference — the frank and heartless unconcern — with which she heard of his return. When she had followed the narrator rather than his story to the end, she languidly called her brothers from the adjoining room. "This gentleman, Mr. Grey, of the 'Argus,' has come across Jim — and Jim is calculating to come here and see father."

The two brothers stared at Grey, slightly shrugged their shoulders with the same utter absence of fraternal sympathy or concern which the girl had shown, and said nothing.

"One moment," said Grey a little warmly; "I have no desire to penetrate family secrets, but would you mind telling me if there is any grave reason why he should not come. Was there any scandalous conduct, unpardonable offense — let us even say — any criminal act on his part which makes his return to this roof impossible?"

The three looked at each other with a dull surprise that ended in a vacant wondering smile. "No, no," they said in one voice. "No, only "—

"Only what?" asked Grey impatiently.

"Dad just hates him!"

"Like pizon," smiled Almira.

The young editor rose with a slight increase of color. "Look here," said the girl, whose dimples had deepened as she keenly surveyed him, as if detecting some amorous artifice under his show of interest for her brother. "Dad's gone down to the sheep-fold and won't be back for an hour. Yo' might bring — *yo' friend* — in."

"He ain't wantin' anything? Ain't dead

broke? nor nothin', eh?" suggested one of the brothers dubiously.

Grey hastened to assure them of Jim's absolute solvency, and even enlarged considerably on his Australian fortune. They looked relieved but not interested.

"Go and fetch him," said the witch, archly hovering near Grey with dancing eyes; "and mind *yo'* come back, too!"

Grey hesitated a moment and then passed out in the dark porch. A dripping figure emerged from the trees opposite. It was Jim.

"Your sister and brothers will see you," said Grey hastily, to avoid embarrassing details. "*He* won't be here for an hour. But I'd advise you to make the most of your time, and get the good-will of your sister." He would have drawn back to let the prodigal pass in alone, but the man appealingly seized his arm, and Grey was obliged to reënter with him. He noticed, however, that he breathed hard.

They turned slightly towards their relative, but did not offer to shake hands with him, nor did he with them. He sat down sideways on an unoffered chair. "The old house got burnt!" he said, wiping his lips, and then drying his wet hair with his hand-kerchief.

As the remark was addressed to no one in particular it was some seconds before the elder brother replied: "Yes."

"Almira's growed."

Again no one felt called upon to answer, and Almira glanced archly at the young editor as if he might have added: "and im-proved."

"You've done well?" returned one of the brothers tentatively.

"Yes, I'm all right," said Jim.

There was another speechless interval. Even the conversational Grey felt under some unhallowed spell of silence that he could not break.

"I see the old well is there yet," said Jim, wiping his lips again.

"Where dad was once goin' to chuck you down for givin' him back talk," said the younger brother casually.

To Mr. Grey's relief and yet astonish-ment, Jim burst into a loud laugh and rubbed his legs. "That's so — how old times *do* come back!"

"And," said the bright-eyed Almira, "there's that old butternut-tree that you shinned up one day when we set the hounds on you. Goodness! how you scooted!"

Again Jim laughed loudly and nodded. "Yes, the same old butternut. How you *do* remember, Almira!" This admiringly,

"And don't you remember Delia Short?" continued Almira, pleased at the admiration, and perhaps a little exalted at the singular attention which the young editor was giving to those cheerful reminiscences. "She, you know, you was reg'larly sick after, so that we always allowed she kinder turned yo' brain afore you went away! Well! all the while you were courtin' her it appears she was secretly married to Jo — yo' friend — Jo Stacy. Lord! there was a talk about that! and about yo' all along thinkin' yo' had chances! Yo' friend here," with an arch glance at Grey, "who 's allus puttin' folks in the newspapers, orter get a hold on that!"

Jim again laughed louder than the others, and rubbed his lips. Grey, however, offered only the tribute of a peculiar smile and walked to the window. "You say your father will return in an hour?" he said, turning to the elder brother.

"Yes, unless he kept on to Watson's."

"Where?" said Jim suddenly.

It struck Grey that his voice had changed —or rather that he was now speaking for the first time in his natural tone.

"Watson's, just over the bridge," explained his brother. "If he went there he won't be back till ten."

Jim picked up his India rubber cape and hat, said, "I reckon I'll just take a turn outside until he gets back," and walked towards the door. None of his relatives moved nor seemed to offer any opposition. Grey followed him quickly. "I'll go with you," he said.

"No," returned Jim with singular earnestness. "You stay here and keep 'em up cheerful like this. They're doing all this for *you*, you know; Almiry's just this chipper only on your account."

Seeing the young man was inflexible, Grey returned grimly to the room, but not until he had noticed, with some surprise, that Jim, immediately on leaving the house, darted off at a quick run through the rain and darkness. Preoccupied with this, and perhaps still influenced by the tone of the previous conversation, he did not respond readily to the fair Almira's conversational advances, and was speedily left to a seat by the fire alone. At the end of ten minutes he regretted he had ever come; when half an hour had passed he wondered if he had not better try to reach the Summit alone. With the lapse of an hour he began to feel uneasy at Jim's prolonged absence in spite of the cold indifference of the household. Suddenly he heard stamping in the porch, a muttered exclamation, and the voices of the two brothers in the hall. "Why, dad! what's up? Yo' look half drowned!"

The door opened upon the sodden, steaming figure of the old man whom he had met on the road, followed by the two sons. But he was evidently more occupied and possessed by some mental passion than by his physical discomfort. Yet strong and dominant over both, he threw off his wet coat and waistcoat as he entered, and marched directly to the fire. Utterly ignoring the presence of a stranger, he suddenly turned and faced his family.

"Half drowned. Yes! and I might have been hull drowned for that matter. The back water of the Fork is all over Watson's, and the bridge is gone. I stumbled onto this end of it in the dark, and went off, head first, into twenty feet of water! Tried to fight my way out, but the current was agin me. I 'd bin down twice, and was going down for the third time, when somebody grabbed me by the scruff o' my neck and under the arm — so! — and swam me to the bank! When I scrambled up I sez: 'I can't see your face,' sez I, 'I don't know who you are,' sez I, 'but I reckon you 're a white man and clear grit,' sez I, ' and there 's my hand on it ! ' And he grabs it and sez, 'We 're quits,' and scooted out o' my sight. And," continued the old man staring at their faces and raising his voice almost to a scream, "who do you think it was? Why, *that sneakin' hound of a brother of yours — Jim!* Jim! the scalla-wag that I booted outer the ranch five years ago, crawlin', writhin' back again after all these years to insult his old father's gray hairs! And some of you — by God — once thought that *I* was hard on him! "

. . . .

The sun was shining brightly the next morning as the young editor halted the up coach in the now dried hollow. As he was clambering to a seat beside the driver, his elbow was jogged at the window. Looking down he saw the face of Jim.

"We had a gay talk last night, remembering old times, did n't we?" said the prodigal cheerfully.

"Yes, but — where are you going now?"

"Back to Australia, I reckon! But it was mighty good to drop in on the old homestead once more!"

"Rather," said the editor, clinging to the window and lingering in mid-air to the manifest impatience of Yuba Bill; "but I say — look here! — were you *quite* satisfied?"

Jim's hand tightened around the young editor's as he answered cheerfully, "Yes." But his face was turned away from the window.

Jane G. Austin.

Standish of Standish.   16mo, $1.25.

Betty Alden.   16mo, $1.25.

A Nameless Nobleman.   16mo, $1.25; paper, 50 cents.

Doctor LeBaron and His Daughters.   16mo, $1.25.

Colonial Novels, including above.   4 vols. $5.00.

The Desmond Hundred.   16mo, $1.00; paper, 50 cents.

David Alden's Daughter, and other Stories. 16mo, $1.25.

Edwin Lassetter Bynner.

Zachary Phips.   16mo, $1.25.

Agnes Surriage.   12mo, $1.25; paper, 50 cents.

The Begum's Daughter.   12mo, $1.25.
These three Historical Novels, 16mo, in box, $3.75.

Penelope's Suitors.   24mo, boards, 50 cents.

Damen's Ghost.   16mo, $1.00; paper, 50 cents.

Harford Flemming.

A Carpet Knight.   16mo, $1.25.

Oliver Wendell Holmes.

Elsie Venner.   New *Riverside Edition.*   Crown 8vo, $1.50.

The Same.   16mo, paper, 50 cents.

The Guardian Angel.   New *Riverside Edition* Crown 8vo, $1.50.

The Same.   16mo, paper, 50 cents.

A Mortal Antipathy.   First Opening of the New Portfolio.   New *Riverside Edition.*   Crown 8vo, gilt top, $1.50.

My Hunt after "The Captain," etc.   Illustrated. 32mo, 75 cents.

HOUGHTON, MIFFLIN & CO., Publishers.

Hans Christian Andersen.

Works.   In ten uniform volumes, 12mo, each $1.00; the set, $10.00; half calf, $25.00.

The Improvisatore; or, Life in Italy.
The Two Baronesses.
O. T.; or, Life in Denmark.
Only a Fiddler.
In Spain and Portugal.
A Poet's Bazaar.   A Picturesque Tour.
Pictures of Travel.
The Story of my Life.   With Portrait.
Wonder Stories told for Children.   Illustrated.
Stories and Tales.   Illustrated.

Mrs. James A. Field.

High-Lights.   16mo, $1.25.

Blanche Willis Howard.

One Summer.   New *Popular Edition*.   Illustrated by Hoppin.   16mo, $1.25.
Aulnay Tower.   12mo, $1.50; paper, 50 cents.
Aunt Serena.   16mo, $1.25; paper, 50 cents.
Guenn.   Illustrated. 12mo, $1.50; paper, 50 cents.
The Open Door.   Crown 8vo, $1.50; paper, 50 cents.

A Fellowe and His Wife.   Collaborated by Blanche Willis Howard and William Sharp.   16mo, $1.25.
No Heroes. A Story for Boys.   Illustrated.   12mo.

Rossiter Johnson (editor).

Little Classics.   18mo, each, $1.00. · The set, in box, $18.00; half calf, or half morocco, $35.00.

1. Exile.	7. Romance.	13. Narrative Poems.
2. Intellect.	8. Mystery.	14. Lyrical Poems.
3. Tragedy.	9. Comedy.	15. Minor Poems.
4. Life.	10. Childhood.	16. Nature.
5. Laughter.	11. Heroism.	17. Humanity.
6. Love.	12. Fortune.	18. Authors.

Virginia W. Johnson.

The House of the Musician.   16mo, paper, 50 cents.

HOUGHTON, MIFFLIN & CO., Publishers.

Sarah Orne Jewett.

The King of Folly Island, and other People. 16mo, $1.25.

Tales of New England. In Riverside Aldine Series. 16mo, $1.00.

A White Heron, and Other Stories. 18mo, $1.25.

A Marsh Island. 16mo, $1.25; paper, 50 cents.

A Country Doctor. 16mo, $1.25.

Deephaven. 18mo, gilt top, $1.25.

Old Friends and New. 18mo, gilt top, $1.25.

Country By-Ways. 18mo, gilt top, $1.25.

The Mate of the Daylight, and Friends Ashore. 18mo, gilt top, $1.25.

Betty Leicester. 18mo, gilt top, $1.25.

Strangers and Wayfarers. 16mo, $1.25.

A Native of Winby. 16mo, $1.25.

William Makepeace Thackeray.

Complete Works. *Illustrated Library Edition.* Including two newly compiled volumes, containing material not hitherto collected in any American or English Edition. With Biographical and Bibliographical Introductions, Portrait, and over 1600 Illustrations. 22 vols. crown 8vo, gilt top, each, $1.50. The set, $33.00; half calf, $60.50; half calf, gilt top, $65.00; half levant, $77.00.

1. Vanity Fair. I.
2. Vanity Fair. II; Lovel the Widower.
3. Pendennis. I.
4. Pendennis. II.
5. Memoirs of Yellowplush, etc.
6. Burlesques.
7. History of Samuel Titmarsh, etc.
8. Barry Lyndon and Denis Duval.
9. The Newcomes. I.
10. The Newcomes. II.
11. Paris Sketch Book, etc.
12. Irish Sketch Book, etc.
13. The Four Georges, etc.
14. Henry Esmond.
15. The Virginians. I.
16. The Virginians. II.
17. Philip. I.
18. Philip. II.; Catherine.
19. Roundabout Papers, etc.
20. Christmas Stories, etc.
21. Contributions to Punch, etc.
22. Miscellaneous Essays.

Thackeray's Lighter Hours. Selections from Thackeray. With Portrait. 32mo, 75 cents.

HOUGHTON, MIFFLIN & CO., Publishers.

William Henry Bishop.

Detmold: A Romance.   18mo, $1.25.

The House of a Merchant Prince.   12mo, $1.25.

Choy Susan, and other Stories.   16mo, $1.25.

The Golden Justice.   16mo, $1.25; paper, 50 cents.

E. W. Howe.

A Man Story.   12mo, $1.50.

The Mystery of the Locks.   New Edition.   16mo, $1.25.

The Story of a Country Town.   New Edition. 16mo, $1.25; paper, 50 cents.

A Moonlight Boy.   With Portrait of the Author. 12mo, $1.50; paper, 50 cents.

Round-Robin Series.

Each volume, 16mo, $1.00; paper, 50 cents.

Damen's Ghost.	The Strike in the B—— Mill.
Madame Lucas.	Fanchette. *Cloth only.*
Leone.	Dorothea. *Cloth only.*
Doctor Ben.	

Ellen Olney Kirk.

Ciphers.   16mo, $1.25.

The Story of Margaret Kent.   New Edition. 16mo, $1.25; paper, 50 cents.

Sons and Daughters.   12mo, $1.25; paper, 50 cents.

Queen Money.   New Edition.   16mo, $1.25; paper, 50 cents.

Better Times.   Stories.   12mo, $1.50.

A Midsummer Madness.   16mo, $1.25; paper, 50 cents.

A Lesson in Love.   16mo, $1.00; paper, 50 cents.

A Daughter of Eve.   12mo, $1.50; paper, 50 cents.

Walford.   16mo, $1.25; paper, 50 cents.

HOUGHTON, MIFFLIN & CO., Publishers.